Libra

24 September – 23 October

DID YOU PURCHASE THIS BOOK WITHOUT A COVER?
If you did, you should be aware it is **stolen property**, as it was reported 'unsold and destroyed' by a retailer.
Neither the author nor the publisher has received any payment for this book.

First published in the Australia New Zealand territory in 2007 by
Harlequin Enterprises Pty Ltd

ABN 47 001 180 918

Level 5, 15 Help Street, Chatswood, NSW 2067 AUSTRALIA.

ISBN 978 0 733 58994 2

Typeset at Midland Typesetters Australia

Printed and bound in Australia by McPhersons Printing Group

About Dadhichi

Dadhichi is one of Australia's foremost astrologers, and is frequently seen on TV and in the media. He has the unique ability to draw from complex astrological theory to provide clear, easily understandable advice and insights for people who want to know what their future may hold.

In the 25 years that Dadhichi has been practising astrology, and conducting face and other esoteric readings, he has provided over 9,000 consultations. His clients include celebrities, political and diplomatic figures and media and corporate identities from all over the world.

Dadhichi's unique blend of astrology and face reading helps people fulfil their true potential. His extensive experience practising western astrology is complemented by his research into the theory and practice of eastern forms of astrology.

Dadhichi has been a guest on many Australian television shows and several of his political and worldwide forecasts have proved uncannily accurate. He has appeared on many of Australia's leading television networks and is a regular columnist for several Australian magazines.

His websites www.astrology.com.au, www.facereader.com and soulmate.com.au which attract hundreds of thousands of visitors each month, offer a wide variety of features, helpful information and services.

Dedicated to The Light of Intuition

Sri V. Krishnaswamy—mentor and friend

With thanks to Julie, Joram, Isaac and Janelle

Welcome from Dadhichi

Dear Friend,

It's a pleasure knowing you're reading this, your astrological forecast for 2009. There's nothing more exciting than looking forward to a bright new year and considering what the stars have in store and how you might make the most of what's on offer in your life.

Apart from the anticipation of what I might predict will happen to you, of what I say about your upcoming luck and good fortune, remember that astrology is first and foremost a tool of personal growth, self-awareness and inner transformation. What 'happens to us' is truly a reflection of what we're giving out; the signals we are transmitting to our world, our universe.

The astrological adage of 'As above, so below' can also be interpreted in a slightly different way when I say 'As within, so without'! In other words, as hard as it is to believe, the world and our experiences of it, or our relationships and circumstances, good or bad, do tend to mirror our own belief systems and mental patterns.

It is for this reason that I thought I'd write a brief introductory note to remind you that the stars are pointers to your wonderful destiny and that you must work with them to realise your highest and most noble goals. The greatest marvel and secret is your own inner self! Astrology reveals these inner secrets of your character, which are the foundation of your life's true purpose.

What is about to happen to you this year is exciting, but what you *do* with this special power of knowledge, how you share your talents with others, and the way you truly enjoy each moment of your life is far more important than knowing *what* will happen. This is the key to a 'superior' kind of happiness. It will start to open up to you when you live in harmony with your true nature as shown by astrology.

I really hope you enjoy your coming twelve months, and gain new insights and fresh perspectives on your life through studying your 2009 horoscope. Here's hoping great success will be yours and health, love and happiness will follow wherever you go.

I leave you now with the words of a wise man, who once said:

Sow a thought, and you reap an act;
Sow an act, and you reap a habit;
Sow a habit, and you reap a character;
Sow a character, and you reap a destiny.
Your thoughts are the architects of your destiny.

Warm regards, and may the stars shine brightly for you in 2009!

Your Astrologer,

Dadhichi Toth

Contents

LIBRA

The Libra Identity

Many people seem to think that success in one area can compensate for failure in other areas. But can it really? ... True effectiveness requires balance.

—Steven Covey

Libra: A Snapshot

Key characteristics

Refined, social, artistic, vacillating, intellectual, communicative, concerned with relationships

Compatible star signs

Gemini, Leo, Sagittarius, Aquarius

Key life phrase

I interact

Platinum assets

Great strength, vitality and magnetism

Life goals

To set an example to others and lead with integrity

Zodiac totem

The Scales of Justice

Zodiac symbol

♎

Zodiac facts

Seventh sign of the zodiac; movable, barren, masculine, dry

Element

Air

Famous Librans

Barbara Walters, Catherine Zeta-Jones, Julio Iglesias, Moon Zappa, Michael Douglas, Will Smith, Olivia Newton-John, Mahatma Gandhi, Gwyneth Paltrow, Richard Harris, Neve Campbell, Sting, David Lee Roth, Alicia Silverstone, Sigourney Weaver, Matt Damon, Roger Moore, John Lennon, Hugh Jackman and Luciano Pavarotti

Key to karma, spirituality and emotional balance

Your key life phrase is 'I interact'. This is because of your inherent ability to deal with people and exchange ideas. Libra is an air sign and this relates to your intellect.

One of your greatest life challenges is to find the appropriate balance between your own needs and the needs of others. You will eventually learn to honour your instincts and not rely too much on what others think or say.

When it comes to making decisions you will eventually develop self-confidence in your own intuition. Don't rely too much on relationships for your emotional or spiritual contentment. Your major karmic lesson will be to deal with these issues.

To open your heart and feel more trusting of your own self, the essential oil jasmine is useful. Wednesdays, Fridays and Saturdays are your best days for connecting with your inner self through meditation and other self-help practices.

Libra: Your profile

Because of your amazing ability to balance so many things, it's a wonder you didn't choose a life as a circus juggler! You are, after all, Libra, represented by the scales, which symbolise judgement and balance. Your sign falls under the category of air, which reflects your superior intellectual development. Being a Libran is synonymous with thinking and you use your mind to solve your own and others' problems. Being the seventh sign of the zodiac, relationships will be your priority and you will primarily project your sense of balance in this area of life.

As a Libran you are the consummate social butterfly and people love being around you. Your ability to communicate is one of your greatest strengths and others often admire your ability to articulate your thoughts so well, even if they don't necessarily come out and tell you so. You're one of the signs of the zodiac who naturally has the gift of the gab. This ability to speak your mind means you're able to mediate or negotiate in virtually any circumstance you find yourself. This doesn't necessarily mean all Librans work in sales or public relations, but your words flow so easily that people would be surprised if you didn't pursue this kind of career.

Being impartial and possessing a talent for seeing all sides of a problem is both a blessing and a curse for you. It makes it hard to reach a decision, which is why Librans are considered one of the most indecisive signs in the zodiac. Another side to this is that you can't stand being disliked and fear offending anyone. Because of this you sometimes ingratiate yourself for the sake of keeping the peace. That would be a shame because you must always speak the truth even if it is unpalatable others.

Make decisions for yourself. At times you need so much feedback that you end up tying yourself in knots, asking everyone else their opinion on your situation or problem. By all means ask others' advice, but weigh up the pros and cons before making your own decisions. This will empower you and you won't feel as ineffectual or dependent on others. On drawing important conclusions you will ultimately be able to say it was your own verdict.

Sharing is one of your other best qualities and, with your wonderful magnetic charm, you never have a problem making friends. People don't always agree with you but you are just so persuasive that it's often hard for them not to agree just because they like you so much. You know how to make others feel comfortable.

Harmony and a peaceful environment are a must if you are to find peace in life. This is to be expected because of your ruling planet Venus dominating your life. This gracious and feminine planet brings out the softer side of your character. You like to express this through your home, furnishings and personal fashion statements.

You're a stylish person and always pride yourself on the fact that good taste is something you should exhibit in everything you do. You tend to have a natural flair for fashion, colour and other artistic pursuits. You're regarded as elegant and tasteful by friends and strangers alike. First impressions are lasting and you understand this principle so success follows you wherever you go. People want to keep in touch with you once they meet you and feel as though you're able to help them also develop a more refined approach in life.

Parties, the good life and anything that brings you in contact with people are what you like to do. Mixing with others and learning about the different characters in life is a lifelong activity that is part of your curiosity for human nature. You truly are a 'people person'. You'll always be surrounded by friends and family.

Venus, your ruler, is the planet of love and this is at the heart of your Libran nature. The search for personal happiness through a meaningful relationship will be your most significant dream. Finding your soulmate will lead you to search high and low for the perfect mate. Because of your loving nature, you shouldn't have too much trouble fulfilling this ambition, as long as you are able to overcome that quality of indecisiveness.

There are three grades of Libra. Which of these do you fall under? You can figure this out by the date of your Libran birth.

If you were born between the 24th of September and the 3rd of October, you epitomise the Libran spirit. This makes you artistic, compassionate and socially engaging. Venus will bring you many friends in life and loving unconditionally will be your greatest quality.

Were you born between the 4th and the 13th of October? Some would say you are harmlessly mad! I say that in the nicest possible way because you are a bundle of fun and at times can be somewhat erratic. You'd like to think that life is meant to be a barrel of surprises and add a touch of spice to any situation.

If you were born between the 14th and the 23rd of October you are the eternal student, constantly on the lookout for knowledge and other facts and figures. You'll never grow tired of learning new things and, because of Mercury's co-rulership, your life will be active and your mind forever young.

Libra role model: Sting

Sting is a Libran, like you. Apart from his music he has also taken an active interest in spiritual and social issues. He is a continuing campaigner for world peace and humanitarian enterprises. He has an extraordinary way of communicating feelings through his music and refined intellect. Sting epitomises the true Libran personality.

Libra: The light side

It's impossible not to love Libra. Venus is the planet that infuses you with charm and grace. Wherever you go, people are enamoured by your bubbly personality, which always brings life and light to any party.

You possess loads of sophistication but always treat people equally and never look down on them. This is why you're loved by others. Because of your ability to connect with people so easily, life will always bring you ample opportunities for luck and good fortune. It's a fact of life that, if you radiate cheer and good vibes, others naturally want to help you.

One of the best features of your character is that of being able to see many sides of a story. Where there is trouble, people turn to you and they trust your ability to give them a fair and unbiased opinion of the true state of the situation. You are calm and sensible, quick and insightful, in the way you offer advice.

Librans have a wonderful sense of humour and are able to use this to their advantage. Great communication skills plus artistic flair with a smattering of humour is a no-brainer combination for all-round success and lifelong contentment.

Libra: The shadow side

No amount of luck or success can hide the fact that some Librans, not all, feel inwardly insecure about themselves. This is quite contradictory because you're such an attractive personality and endear everyone to you. You never quite believe that what you have to offer is good enough and are constantly seeking others' approval. Feeling like this is not necessary; you should be satisfied in your own abilities without needing the crutch of other people's opinions.

The other difficulty you have is sometimes agreeing to do more than you are capable of delivering. You don't want turn anyone down, but in the process will undermine your own reputation and credibility by not making good your promises. Try to remain a little more aware of your limitations and don't be afraid to say no when you realise you can't possibly please everyone.

Because you love sharing your successes with the world, you mustn't be seen to be boastful about your achievements. You are sometimes unaware that some people feel you are bragging and not necessarily generously giving of yourself. You will alienate people rather than drawing them closer to you. Try to remain a little more tight-lipped about your achievements.

Libra woman

You were born under the attractive rays of Venus, which make you loving, graceful and attractive. Venus is the most feminine planet of the zodiac and represents your true nature. You are indeed feminine, through and through. You don't have to do too much to make others stand up and take notice. Your Libran personality is captivating even on the most average day.

You have a taste for soft fabrics, relaxing environments, perfumes and anything that can make you feel and look better. You also like to make others feel good, too. Bringing harmony to the world is your life mission and through these accessories you're able to spread happiness everywhere.

Venus is also the planet that signifies love and for you there is nothing more important than finding the perfect partner. This is at the top of the list of your life's priorities, but often it's not that easy for you to achieve. You have high ideals and want someone who will treat you as an equal, not just as a woman. These ideals are not easily met by the men you encounter and so you may have to wait a little longer than most to meet 'Mr Right'.

You are keenly interested in relationships of all sorts and what makes men and women tick. You enjoy discussing the psychology of partnerships and love and have a reasonably good grasp of what makes a successful relationship. You work hard in your relationships and in particular those of a romantic nature because, when things are going smoothly in this part of your life, you feel at your best. Your partner will be the luckiest person to be the recipient of your good will and affection.

Don't try too hard to be accepted as this could cause you to go to extremes. Earlier in your life you had a tendency to be a little hedonistic, perhaps because you wanted to be loved. You may push yourself way too hard but now hopefully you have become more settled in yourself and accepting of who you are. You still suffer self-doubt from time to time. Don't let people's comments affect you personally. Don't be so sensitive about passing remarks.

Some Libran women are afraid of being alone because they are so accustomed to being with others. It's a great idea to spend some time alone in meditation to get to know yourself. Ultimately you are your own best friend and this goes a long way to ensuring you're comfortable when people aren't around.

Because of your instinct for justice and fair play, you sometimes involve yourself in situations you shouldn't. If you see an injustice, you're the first to come to someone's rescue, only to find yourself becoming embroiled in something way over your head. You need to be less impulsive before rescuing others or you're likely to become the victim yourself.

You have an instinctive ability to come up with solutions for difficult problems and these quick fixes are often on the tip of your tongue, much to the surprise of those who rely on your assistance to solve many of their complex issues. Librans really are not given credit for the compassionate and selfless help they offer.

Libra is the sign of balance and is represented by the scales. You know full well that most of your life lessons are centred on balance. The best way you can do this is to utilise your artistic and aesthetic skills together. This makes you feel calm and in tune with yourself and the universe. It will soothe your soul and bring you the balance you desire.

Libra man

The Libran male is all class, thanks to the balancing and attractive influence of the ruling planet, Venus.

Endowed with sensitivity and intuitive connection to your own feminine nature, being born under this sign is indeed lucky. You have an innate understanding of human nature, and women in particular relate to this rare quality of yours.

You have a charming way about you, which makes you attractive and easy to get along with. In fact, sometimes it's probably too easy to get along with you so people could be forgiven for wondering whether you are simply ingratiating yourself with them just to be accepted. In some cases this may in fact be true and you must be careful not to mix up diplomacy with insecurity about being rejected.

Libran men sometimes encounter difficulties with women because they are so easily enamoured by them. You probably have many friends of the same sex but equally as many women. You relate to women's issues and can easily see things from their perspective. Some men probably wonder why you're always surrounded by females. Just tell them they'll have to ask Venus, your ruling planet, which makes this all possible. On the other hand, your partner or spouse may not take too kindly to this and you will have to find a happy balance between your personal life and the numerous friendships you juggle.

Libran men have a great sense of humour and wit. You are impromptu in the way you come up with words. Butter wouldn't melt in your mouth. You know exactly what to say at exactly the right time for maximum impact. Being born under the air sign means you have a command of language; and not just words, for you also understand how language impacts upon others and use this to your advantage.

You're well up to date on current affairs and other newsworthy items so you are never boring to be with. You have a broad base of knowledge in scientific, cultural and spiritual areas and surprise others with the depth of your wisdom. You enjoy learning and will never stop absorbing facts and information, which to you is essential in becoming an all-round, useful human being.

Relationships fascinate you and, although you know everything about them, you are sometimes still unfulfilled because of your high expectations. Your ideals are sometimes quite unrealistic so you must endeavour to be more practical to by accepting the natural flaws in others' personalities. This could lead you to an eternal search for the perfect partner who, as you know, is highly unlikely to exist. In long-term relationships, you must be absolutely certain that you play the field long enough before making any permanent commitment.

Making decisions is one of the most difficult parts of being Libran. Once you learn to trust your own mind you will overcome this issue and can expect your personal and business life much to be much more successful and fulfilling. Once you've made up your mind, stick to your decision.

Libra child

You're fortunate to have in your company a child born under the sign of Libra. The lulling and affectionate vibrations of Venus are found equally in both boys and girls of this sign.

Your Libran child will grow into being a great friend to you. Through this reciprocal relationship you will also learn a lot about life. Because of their charm and vivacious energy, their social life will become an important facet of their personalities and you will to want to be part of that. They love parties, group activities and anything that gives them the opportunity to shine among their peers. It's also not a bad idea to make your child part of the adult conversational group. This is a great way to help them develop more mature communications skills.

Children of Libra are wonderful communicators and speak at an early age. You should be prepared to get into long conversations with them, even in their earlier years, because their intelligence is quite well-developed for their age. Due to this you will need to give them plenty of activities to occupy their curious brains and make sure you also have the book of *How, Where and Why*? handy to answer their never-ending questions about this, that or the other.

Your Libran child is quite artistic and this also will be evident from an early age. Their musical, painting and drawing skills will amaze you. They also have a wonderful sense of perspective and so you should help them to develop these talents when and wherever possible.

A child of Libra is sometimes highly strung because they are born under the element of air. Gently encourage them in the art of relaxation and make the above creative activities part of their daily routine. This will help them unwind and develop a greater sense of poise and balance, which is, after all, what the sign of Libra is all about.

These children respond best to love and affection, not harsh words. If you must reprimand them, always do so in a firm but loving manner. If you are too heavy-handed with them, they are likely to retreat into their shell and become introverted.

Teaching Libran children good dietary habits is not a bad idea to help balance their inquisitive little minds. It is better for them to eat smaller meals several times a day than fewer, larger meals.

Romance, love and marriage

Love and sensuality are the most natural things for Libra. It is part and parcel of who you are. Relationships dominate your each and every move in life. Most Librans would prefer to be unhappily in love than not in love at all, and herein lies both your greatest strength as well as weakness when it comes to relationships.

You have an innate affection, which makes you valued as a friend and lover. You constantly go to great lengths to demonstrate just how much you love another; but remember, familiarity breeds contempt and often your desire to give love is perceived as a form of insecurity and results in exactly the opposite. Try not to be so needy and, once you've found a partner, give them some room to breathe because your brand of love can sometimes be a little smothering, to say the least.

You have a tendency to dive in boots and all once you feel you've met your perfect soulmate. But on occasion you're impulsive and may not know enough about the other person before committing your body, mind and spirit to them. Try to get to know them a little more before declaring your love. You can do this through those activities that are dearest to your heart such as music, dance, painting, theatre and other social get-togethers. This is where you can learn about your lover, taking your time to first understand their true personality rather than trying to fill some gap in your heart.

For Libra it is very important to be able to switch off from relationships, at least temporarily and most importantly, when a relationship is going through a rough patch. You have a tendency to take these emotional and romantic problems into other areas of your life, which can make you dysfunctional, particularly at work. You need a strategy that will allow you occupy yourself with other things until you can solve these love issues.

You're a loyal person but only when you feel the other person has made a firm commitment to you as well. Until you feel that another person's loyalty is undying, you will play the field and enjoy the chase. Mars and the sign of Aries regulate your marriage zone and this makes you passionate in your affairs. The demonstration of love is essential to you, so you will constantly be proving your own feelings to your partner or demanding that they prove their love to you. This can get little tiring, particularly if your spouse or partner is not as expressive as you are. Learn to accept other gestures of love that are not necessarily tactile.

In matters of intimacy you feel that exploration is part of the deal. You need someone who is prepared to make love a journey, not just a thought. You want to spend your life with someone who will be equally adventurous and excited about the prospect of getting to know you; not just in the first instance, but continually as the relationship grows. The worst thing for a Libran is for boredom to set in. The partner of Libra should be completely aware that should this happen a Libran cannot remain without love and will more than likely consider other possibilities.

Choose your partner well and make certain that they listen to you when you have something important to say. Some Libran women become disenchanted by their relationships for this reason. The complaint is that their partner doesn't share their feelings or thoughts with them and this is completely frustrating. In your over-enthusiasm to race up to the altar, you must take the preliminary precautions to consider how compatible you are with another person. Generally Librans get on well with everyone; however, marriage and long-term commitment is a whole new ball game. Please be patient and take your time in choosing well.

In marriage Libra chooses to create a safe and nurturing environment for their family. Once married, Librans like a financially and materially secure home base in which to rear children. You'll spend a lot of time creating a harmonious environment that will allow you the peace of mind to execute your duties fully as a spouse and parent.

Health, wellbeing and diet

Health can be a rollercoaster ride for Librans due to the influence of Venus, which can at times makes you feel completely full of energy and life yet at other times unmotivated and lethargic. Venus is astrologically well known as the planet that causes excessive eating and living habits. Overindulgence is one of the key words for this planet and is specifically the area that may affect you and your health.

Being sensitive by nature, you are able to tune in to your body's signals, which is the best barometer of your health you can follow. Listen to what is being 'said' and adjust your lifestyle accordingly.

Because you are an air sign, your thinking often underlies many of your health issues. Over-thinking and worry and are tied in with your star sign and may lead to discomfort and disease in the long term if you don't control these patterns.

Your kidneys and bladder are constitutional weak points for your birth sign. Eating organic and fresh fruits and vegetables will help keep your system clear of any toxins, which could overload these organs. Of course, drinking plenty of water and freshly squeezed juices will also help maintain optimum health.

It's preferable for you to eat several smaller meals throughout the day rather than larger ones. Due to your metabolic rate you burn calories quickly and need to feed yourself more frequently. This will optimise your energy levels and generally make you feel better.

Of course, processed foods are out of the question. If you are a meat eater, lean meats like chicken or veal will enhance your health, vitality and general wellbeing.

Your ruling planet Venus is fair in colour and so food ruled by her should be eaten. Fruits and vegetables such as honeydew melon, bananas, rice, raw milk and yoghurt are excellent sources of vitamins and minerals. As a substitute for sugar you can try the South American herb stevia, which also acts as a tonic and antibiotic.

Processed meats such as ham and salami should be avoided due to the chemical additives. Apart from the negative effects on your body, chemicals can affect your emotions and cause mood swings. Keep a record of what you eat and study how you feel from the different foods you consume. This will be an eye-opener for you.

Work

Work is a big part of your life and affords you the opportunity to mingle with people, share ideas and work towards common goals with them. Money is important to you but not as important as the work itself.

You like mental challenges and jobs that are stimulating. You like a social setting to express your ideas and make valuable contributions.

It is vital that your workplace is harmonious and the people you work with offer you the respect you deserve. If this is the case you will perform your professional duties well and can achieve success.

The fields of communication, teaching, sales and marketing are excellent areas for Librans to make their mark on the world. You have an intuitive understanding of what others want and therefore you approach work from the point of view of serving others as best you can. They appreciate this and reciprocate by giving you the support you require.

Being ruled by Venus, the artistic planet, also hints at the fact you'll do well in the aesthetic fields such as music, dance, choreography, film and television, industrial design and interior decoration. Architectural and building careers are often found to be appealing to those born under Libra.

Your lucky days

Your luckiest days are Wednesday, Friday and Saturday.

Your lucky numbers

Remember that the forecasts given later in the book will help you optimise your chances of winning. Your lucky numbers are:

6, 15, 24, 33, 42, 51

8, 17, 26, 35, 44, 53

5, 14, 23, 32, 41, 50

Your destiny years

Your most important years are 6, 15, 24, 33, 42, 51, 60, 78 and 87.

LIBRA

Star Sign Compatibility

The Eskimos had fifty-two names for snow because it was important to them; there ought to be as many for love.

—Margaret Atwood

Romantic compatibility

How compatible are you with your current partner, lover or friend? Did you know that astrology can reveal a whole new level of understanding between people simply by looking at their star sign and that of their partner? In this chapter I'd like to share some special insights that will help you better appreciate your strengths and challenges using Sun sign compatibility.

The Sun reflects your drive, willpower and personality. The essential qualities of two star signs blend like two pure colours producing an entirely new colour. Relationships, similarly, produce their own emotional colours when two people interact. The following is a general guide to your romantic prospects with others and how, by knowing the astrological 'colour' of each other, the art of love can help you create a masterpiece.

When reading the following I ask you to remember that no two star signs are ever *totally* incompatible. With effort and compromise, even the most 'difficult' astrological matches can work. Don't close your mind to the full range of life's possibilities! Learning about each other and ourselves is the most important facet of astrology.

Each star sign combination is followed by the elements of those star signs and the result of their combining. For instance, Aries is a fire sign and Aquarius is an air sign, and this combination produces a lot of 'hot air'. Air feeds fire, and fire warms air. In fact, fire requires air. However, not all air and fire combinations work. I have included information about the different birth periods within each star sign and this will throw even more light on your prospects for a fulfilling love life with any star sign you choose.

Good luck in your search for love, and may the stars shine upon you in 2009!

Compatibility quick reference guide

Each of the twelve star signs has a greater or lesser affinity with one another. The quick reference guide on page 30 will show you who's hot and who's not so hot as far as your relationships are concerned.

LIBRA + ARIES

Air + Fire = Hot air

Libra and Aries together make a 'love bomb'. The fire sign of Aries is the astrological opposite of your own Libran sign. Some astrologers believe this combination is a pretty good one; however, while opposites generally do attract, Aries may also be a challenge in a relationship.

Aries is so fiery and often 'in your face' in their interactions with people. Decisive and upfront by nature, they like to act first, speak next, and think last. The raging Aries' fire knows no stillness and this is because their star sign is also movable by nature.

You are not as decisive in making up your mind and so Aries becomes impatient with you and will let you know it, too. You're constantly holding back while they will forge forward with or without you. And forget about diplomacy—they want to be right all the time. This will be irritating for you.

Aries is like a dog at a bone and sticks to one viewpoint whereas you're balanced in judgement and see more than one side to the story. Aries is impulsive in letting others know

Quick reference guide: Horoscope compatibility between signs (percentage)

	Aries	Taurus	Gemini	Cancer	Leo	Virgo	Libra	Scorpio	Sagittarius	Capricorn	Aquarius	Pisces
Aries	60	65	65	65	90	45	70	80	90	50	55	65
Taurus	60	70	70	80	70	90	75	85	50	95	80	85
Gemini	70	70	75	60	80	75	90	60	75	50	90	50
Cancer	65	80	60	75	70	75	60	95	55	45	70	90
Leo	90	70	80	70	85	75	65	75	95	45	70	75
Virgo	45	90	75	75	75	70	80	85	70	95	50	70
Libra	70	75	90	60	65	80	80	85	80	85	95	50
Scorpio	80	85	60	95	75	85	85	90	80	65	60	95
Sagittarius	90	50	75	55	95	70	80	85	85	55	60	75
Capricorn	50	95	50	45	45	95	85	65	55	85	70	85
Aquarius	55	80	90	70	70	50	95	60	60	70	80	55
Pisces	65	85	50	90	75	70	50	95	75	85	55	80

their opinion even if they don't particularly know what they're talking about. This can be embarrassing because you prefer to be armed with information before you open your mouth. You're quite sympathetic to differing opinions. You would like Aries to be the same, but it's hard for them to make concessions.

You're quite sociable and thrive on cordial conversation with all sorts of people. Aries will indeed stimulate your communication but is mentally black and white. Essentially, you are quite different people and your personalities often clash.

But let's not throw the baby out with the bathwater just yet! Although air and fire are quite different elements, they mutually support each other. Air feeds and intensifies fire, and fire heats and stirs air.

There are significant connections between fire and air and this means the two of you will make a positive impression on each other, if you choose to. Aries must be more patient because there's certainly a great connection sexually. In this area you will both find happiness. You will no doubt stoke the raging Arian fires and offer them many pleasurable hours in the bedroom. The feeling will be mutual.

The success of this relationship depends on the pace and level of comfort you develop over time.

Exciting and tender lovemaking is on the cards in a relationship with Aries born between 21 and 30 March. You'll feel an instant attraction the moment you meet them. These Aries born are strong willed but also protect your family interests if you choose to make a life with them.

If you are attracted to an Aries born between 31 March and 10 April, more than likely you will find that they will become great friends rather than romantic lovers.

With Aries born between 11 April and 20 April, an intellectual rapport is likely. However, even though you'll probably have much to talk about, there is still a gap that may be difficult to bridge in your basic philosophies.

LIBRA + TAURUS

Air + Earth = Dust

Both of you are ruled by the same planet, namely Venus, which is a great basis for this relationship. You'll find yourself immediately attracted to Taurus because of this. However, the way Venus operates through Libra and Taurus is quite different, but with your great communications skills and diplomacy and the earthy, practical nature of Taurus, there is a formidable match.

With your similarities in your love of social activity, partying and generally having a good time with friends and family, this is an extra bonus. Taurus in particular loves home and domestic life, so it's not a bad idea to combine these areas of activity and hang out with others. Taurus does, however, need a quieter and slower lifestyle than you.

Because you like peace, harmony and a gentle environment, Taurus will satisfy you in this respect as they move a little more slowly and are not impulsive. They like to think through their decisions before acting on them and this fits in with your sometimes indecisive nature. Therefore here is another big plus for both of you in moving forward together in life.

You are sensitive to Taurus's needs, and can support them to their satisfaction, which will ensure a rich and mutually satisfying relationship for you both. This will be a partnership in which you'll both nurture each other.

You're the thinker of the team and Taurus is probably more of a doer. With the combination of air and earth you can move mountains and achieve much in life. You'll probably need to be more stable to make Taurus feel secure. You will inspire Taurus in their life goals and the direction in which they're going; you'll be good at giving them the advice as well as the gentle push they need. This will invigorate them to reciprocate and satisfy you financially.

In the extreme there can be a conflict between personal and social obligations, which might mean you're not ready to settle down together. Allowances will need to be made on both sides. If you end up surrendering to Taurus's needs out of a sense of obligation, your emotional state will suffer. Try adjusting your timetables by respectfully making room for each other.

You can fall head over heels in love with Taureans born between 21 April and 29 April. They are traditional and romantic at heart and will certainly stimulate your physical passions and need for love and affection.

Taurus individuals born between 30 April and 10 May will also quite in tune with you. The problem with them is that they are a little preoccupied with financial security and may demand an extra effort from you. Carefully work out money objectives with them first before committing.

Taureans born between 11 and 21 May are a little too slow in their thinking and this will probably be a challenge for you. It will be difficult to get them up and out of their inflexible way of seeing and doing things.

LIBRA + GEMINI

Air + Air = Wind

It appears that fortune smiles upon you in this combination. When two air signs come together, what you have is a perfect blend of elements. This is intellectually inspiring for both of you and should be a good omen for the long term.

The planets Venus and Mercury rule Libra and Gemini respectively and are great friends in the planetary scheme. You and Gemini will more than likely enjoy not only a great friendship together but can develop this into a romantic union as well. Air signs are associated with the mind, so Gemini will resonate well with your personality and will easily fulfil your thirst for learning and communication. In this relationship you will learn a great deal from and will act as teachers or guides for each other. The combination of Libra and Gemini is a karmic one. You'll know that without me telling you.

Socialising will be the cornerstone of your relationship as you both need to be with others in creative environments. You'll both enjoy theatre and may even be actively involved in art. Gemini is a restless sign, however, and, being ruled by Mercury, is hard to pin down. You like the fact that they are versatile and interesting people, but they are a little frenetic at times.

There's never a dull moment with Libra and Gemini. You both like to feel as though you are achieving something in life will always be actively engaged in some activity or another. Together you will enjoy each other's company and be constantly amused and attracted by the other. For the most part you are sexually compatible and there will be a touch of fun and playfulness to your lovemaking. Both of you find comfort, warmth and reciprocal affection in this relationship. This does appear to be a special sort of relationship and will be quite obvious when you first meet.

Geminis born between 22 May and 1 June are very attracted to you and you'll feel well suited to them. You'll enjoy spending time with them, but don't get carried away. Before getting too involved, it's not a bad idea to discuss what your long-term plans are because theirs could be a bit nebulous.

Expect an excellent romantic combination with any Gemini born between 2 June and 12 June. The planet Venus brings out their affection and love—and their interest in marriage—as it influences them, too. They are highly affectionate people. You'll also be attracted to their very clever sense of humour.

Geminis born between 13 June and 21 June will give you plenty of excitement and provide you lots of social activity. They are very much attuned to your own spirit and this could be regarded as a near perfect match. You will want to do unusual things together and visit non-traditional places. Culture will be an important link between you as well.

LIBRA + CANCER

Air + Water = Rain

This may not necessarily be the easiest of astrological combinations romantically, but don't lose heart. We must always look at the positive aspects. I say difficult because the signs of Libra and Cancer are at celestial right-angles. This can be one of the most challenging matches of the zodiac, but if you remain aware and are prepared to consummate your love, this might work out for you.

Both of you are primarily interested in fostering peace and harmony in your personal and domestic lives, so they are important common personality traits. Cancer values private and family affairs so this may clash with your endless desire to be the life of the party. You love variety whereas Cancer cherishes the tried and tested. But, it's not the same in every case, as you'll see from some of the different types of Cancer, below. As long as they don't smother you or demand you live your life their way, you'll be able to adapt.

Because of your tremendously vivid imagination, and the fact that Cancer is caring and giving by nature, there is opportunity for both of you to create something wonderful; not just in the relationship, but in your business and family lives as well. This can be a mutually powerful relationship on many levels if you don't let the little things get in the road.

The intimacy level between Libra and Cancer is quite high because of the sympathy between the feminine planets that rule you: the Moon and Venus. At heart you both want to be loved and to express your love, so you will both feel you're being nurtured and appreciated in your relationship. Your partnership therefore has some very positive things going for it, but don't get bogged down in the differences.

If you team up with a Cancer born between 22 June and 3 July, be aware that they are very sensitive. They will offer you love and emotional support, but they are also extremely moody, not unlike yourself at times. This could make your partnership an unpredictable one. They are great friends, however, and friendship will also be a strong point for both of you.

One of the better arrangements would be with Cancerians born between 4 and 13 July. They are ruled by Scorpio, which means they are intensely passionate but also possessive. They share many of your interests, and they're willing to set aside time to focus on you, which will make you very satisfied.

You have strong emotional and karmic bonds with any Cancer born between 14 July and 23 July. This is also a fortunate combination and will offer you valuable life lessons that will cause important transformations in your personality. You too can support these Cancers in a way that will help them develop their own personalities and spiritual potential. There is also a good financial connection. Try to remain open to them.

LIBRA + LEO

Air + Fire = Hot air

This is a relationship that will be based on mateship and true camaraderie. It means you like each other first and foremost, which, as we all know, is just as important as loving each other. The Libra and Leo combination offers you friendship as well as passion and love. When air and fire come together, it's usually pretty special and mutually satisfying on any mental, emotional and physical level.

You are both quite sociable in nature and enjoy being with others. Together you could bring a special warmth and energy to your family and social lives. Because you also both have broad and interesting views on life, you're able to adapt to any situation and might even enjoy travelling together and settling down in different locations to explore the world and enjoy adventures in foreign lands.

There is a natural attraction between you, and you do find the magnetic and vibrant personality of Leo quite irresistible. They are attracted to your mind and the graceful way in which you conduct yourself. They are a little more inflexible in their viewpoints but by the same token are quite enamoured with your ability to bend and stretch your opinions and to swap sides in an argument at will. They find this a little curious but amusing.

Leo is brutally honest and doesn't possess the same diplomacy as you. You respect Leo's honesty but would prefer them to sugar-coat their opinions rather than steamrolling everyone in their path with their brand of truth. You don't like abrasiveness of any sort, even if it wins an argument. This could become a continuing problem for you.

Your attraction to each other is undeniable. People will say 'These two are really well suited' and this will spur you on. You really do make a great couple. Your combined energies create a unique charisma, which draws others to you. This ensures luck and good fortune. You'll both have common interests that include hosting personal and professional functions and parties.

You will enjoy a great friendship and the prospect of marriage with Leos born between 24 July and 4 August. You'll be very attracted to them and enjoy their unique line of thinking as well as their fierce independence.

Your life might become destabilised if you enter into relationship with a Leo born between 5 August and 14 August. The Sagittarian–Jupiter influence present here creates a great deal of change for you and, if travelling is not particularly your cup of tea, you might want to pass on this one. These Leos are always on the go; they will tire you out after a while unless you're prepared to travel with them.

Generally speaking, you and Leo get on very well on a sexual level. However, this last group of Leos will excite you even more if they are born between 15 and 23 August. Aries and Mars co-rule these people, so this brings their passion to the fore. You will have a great friendship and sexual enjoyment with them.

LIBRA + VIRGO

Air + Earth = Dust

The shy and sometimes retiring Virgo personality could become an enjoyable pastime for you when you team up with them. With your exciting and outgoing personality, you will be constantly working at chilling out the highly strung Virgo. Slowly but surely you will be able to bring them to a more relaxed level and then start to see the light and less finicky side of their personality.

Your planets Venus and Mercury are very friendly so there is a natural connection between you, offering a great deal of common interests. Virgo has a penchant for analysing virtually everything you say and initially this could be great conversation, but they start to wear thin when you have to explain every single detail over and over again. This will require much patience on your part. But, you do respect and admire their incredibly fine mental qualities. Virgos are well known for this. Virgos make some of the most interesting conversationalists. When they do choose a topic of interest they go into it with total focus.

You enjoy the inquisitiveness of Virgo but once they start to become regularly critical of you, you'll draw the line. Most Librans are quite able to handle the constructive criticism that Virgo is prone to go through because they understand that this is a way to improve themselves. You always try to see both sides of an argument. Because of this and your wonderful ability to listen, Virgo will respect you and hopefully give up trying to change you, accepting you for who you are.

You are easygoing by nature. You love spontaneous action, but usually Virgo has a plan that is fixed. Sometimes they just won't budge. A great deal of adjustment is necessary so that your lifestyles fit. You need to travel to other worlds, and Virgo should give you a free rein.

You like to explore your sexual nature and Virgo will have to learn to accept this because they are generally more intellectual than physical at the outset. Once they feel secure with you, however, you'll realise that they too have strong sexual needs that need to be met. Virgo requires a structured and formal friendship initially before getting too involved. These points of difference will be far more marked with some types of Virgos than others.

Virgos born between 24 August and 2 September are a very good match for you and are not as critical as many other

Virgos. Communication with them will flow easily and they are emotional creatures as well.

A more serious class of Virgos are those born between 3 September and 12 September and won't enjoy social life as much as you do. They are not as receptive to meeting people and being in groups as you are. Think carefully before getting into a relationship with them.

Virgos born between 13 September and 23 September could be ideally suited to you. They are more tactile and sexually responsive. They are also progressive sexually, which will suit you down to the ground.

LIBRA + LIBRA

Air + Air = Wind

In this relationship, who is going to step up and be the hero when it comes to making a decision? You see, Libra being a movable air sign finds it extremely difficult to come to a conclusion. With both of you to-ing and fro-ing, you might find yourselves dancing around in circles ad infinitum with nothing ever getting done. This is an area where the Librans partnership will need plenty of work, that's for sure. A least one of you will have to be the decision maker and stick to your guns.

One of the solutions is not to take on too much—to do things one step at a time in consultation together (not too much consultation, though)—and this will decompress the situation and help you both become more decisive and responsible as a couple.

Because you both want to live a harmonious life, neither of you will want to upset the applecart by raising issues that you think might get the other offside. This is a mistake and you should always speak about how you feel without fear of offending each other. You are both honest and shouldn't have any problem making the relationship successful.

You live hectic lives with busy social and professional schedules and might find yourselves at odds trying to spend time together. A relationship requires quality time so that it can grow and nurture your inner emotional needs, which are strong. Please note I said 'quality' time, not necessarily 'quantity'. As long as you spend a little time together getting to know each other, the Libra–Libra match does have a chance of working.

By being easygoing, you fit easily into each other's lifestyle once you decide to make a firm commitment. You share a love of harmony and beauty, and this will elevate your relationship and create some truly special feelings between you. You will provide each other warmth, affection and physical intimacy. With your astrological mirror image, there should be plenty of mutual affection, especially sexually.

By and large, compatibility between people of the same star sign is either superb or doomed to utter failure. For Libra it depends on how capable you are of finding balance, especially in the decision-making area.

If you're looking for true love, Librans born between 24 September and 3 October will quite likely fulfil your dreams. Venus promises love and fondness with these people. There's no doubt your intimate moments will be appreciated by both of you.

A relationship that is out of the ordinary, unexpected and surprising is likely with Librans born between 4 October and 13 October. Don't expect a typical day-to-day life with them, though, as they want excitement as a permanent feature of life.

You have an instant intellectual bond with Librans born between 14 October and 23 October. These people are very much in tune with you, and you will spend hours sharing your thoughts and brainstorming. Good humour is a key ingredient of their personalities.

LIBRA + SCORPIO

Air + Water = Rain

Libra–Scorpio is an intense match so you'll need to be resilient to handle the highs and lows of a dynamic relationship with the Scorpion. Passion is the keyword here, with your ruling planet, Venus, and their Mars–Pluto rulers combining to create a relationship you'll never forget.

Scorpio is very enamoured by your sensual, sensitive yet intelligent personality, and you'll find yourself wanting more and more of the powerful Scorpio in your life. This partnership might become addictive to you, especially on the physical side. Scorpio is intriguing so be careful how you become involved with them. There may be something secretive about your relationship because Scorpio is probably the most secretive sign of all. With Libra this may be more evident than with other signs.

Scorpio is possessive and often jealous in love. They demand absolute loyalty and, because you are a free spirit, Scorpio will have to deal with this and it won't be easy for them. Basically, they are all-or-nothing lovers, so get used to it.

The fact that you are an air element means you will be fascinated by the reflective and mystical Scorpio. You will both develop a wonderful level of communication and understanding and this will trigger spiritual and philosophical insights for you. Scorpio is keenly interested in the underlying power of life and death and human nature. This will attract you and bring you closer together.

There is powerful sexual energy between Libra and Scorpio. The archetypal Mars and Venus combination says it all. But, they also say that women are from Venus and men are from Mars. These are sometimes diametrically opposed forces and at the same time compelled to be drawn together into love and passion. That very much sums up your relationship with Scorpio.

If you're planning a committed relationship with a Scorpio, your financial prospects are very good. You will be able to earn money together and will enjoy each other's company doing it. You may, however, have to concede to Scorpio and allow them to a least believe that they rule the roost financially. Your diplomacy will know how to do that quite well without humiliating yourself in the process.

An excellent relationship can be expected with Scorpios born between 24 October and 2 November. These Scorpios are cusp natives, so they also display some of your own Libran traits. This is therefore a good mental and sexual union.

There could be a few problems with Scorpios born between 3 November and 12 November, as Jupiter and Neptune cause karmic rifts and challenges between you. The lesson for you two now will be to give and take and, if you are the one giving more than you are receiving, you might not want to pursue this any further.

Get ready for a few highs and lows if you enter into a relationship with Scorpios born between 13 and 22 November. They have the unpredictable Moon influencing their emotions. You might need someone a little more stable to balance your own changeable moods.

LIBRA + SAGITTARIUS

Air + Fire = Hot air

A relationship between Libra and Sagittarius is really like a breath of fresh air. This too is a very good combination astrologically, even though your ruling planets are not necessarily the best of friends. Still, Venus and Jupiter, your ruling planets respectively, do indicate fortunate events in life and on some level at least you can expect some very good fortune by joining forces.

Both of you feel comfortable in each other's company and your communication flows very easily. You feel friendly with each other and Sagittarius confides in you and feels naturally nurtured by your open and supportive ways. Although the Sagittarian is often a little outspoken and blunt in manner, you of all star signs is able to refine them and bring out their best potential as human beings.

There are some very interesting similarities between you and most notably that has to do with adventure and a desire to experience more of life. Sagittarians love variety, change and exploration no less than you do. Your Sagittarian partner will more than likely provide you all the excitement and diversity that you desire and so your time together will not only be fun but enlightening.

Travelling to exciting destinations, enjoying nature and wildlife will be a common thread upon which many of your activities will hinge. In fact, some Librans and Sagittarians come together while holidaying, travelling overseas or interstate ... or, in some cases, in transit or shopping at the local mall!

The romantic side of your relationship is full of warmth and generosity. Sex is more primal with the fiery Sagittarius; but, as I've already mentioned, air (Libra) stimulates fire and you'll enjoy this even though you might not readily admit it!

Sagittarius must be careful not to push you too far too soon. You are sensitive and want someone who exhibits good taste and manners. However, once you start to relax and get to know each other, your closeness will move to a deeper level and your satisfaction will increase.

Sagittarians born between 23 November and 1 December have fairly large egos, but once you get over this initial hurdle you'll find them quite intriguing—even attractive—so there's no harm in trying it on. You might slowly begin to warm to them.

Your best Sagittarian companion would be someone born between 2 December and 11 December. They are strongly controlled by Mars and Aries. They are hot-headed individuals and tend to shoot from the hip as well as being constantly on the go. You'll need lots of physical energy to keep up with them. Oodles of sport are on the agenda with this match.

You will have a great relationship with Sagittarians born between 12 and 22 December. These characters are genuinely caring and attentive to your needs, even though they appear to have rather big egos. Don't judge them too quickly; if you do, you may miss out on their special brand of love.

LIBRA + CAPRICORN

Air + Earth = Dust

Pity is never a basis for a good relationship, so if you feel sorry for Capricorn because they appear a little too solemn or withdrawn, wake up. Capricorn doesn't need your pity. But they do need your love, and that is something you can give them due to your abundance of warm and genuine emotions, which are endowed on you by Venus. At first it might not seem like a Libra–Capricorn combination is likely to work, but that is a superficial view. Actually, this is a good combination.

With Capricorn, you must remember that love is an extension of security. Generally they are not frivolous and they might misinterpret your love of socialising as just that. They need airtight guarantees and you will therefore have to assure them that your love and support is in no way compromised by desire for outside friendships. You might find their attitude is controlling, but this is something you may have to live with because it is a component of Capricorn's personality.

Capricorn likes to feel and touch things, preferably expensive things. You don't mind this at all because you too have a fine taste and the desire for as much luxury as possible. Because of this you can work in tandem to create the most beautiful environment in which to make your life together. The Libran–Capricorn combination is usually successful on a material level. Both of you will enjoy a good level of security in each other's arms.

Capricorn is sometimes a workaholic and this could produce a rift between you. You need to set boundaries at the outset if your Capricorn is more wedded to their work than they are to you. Use some of that Libran charm to woo them. You will enjoy the benefits that Capricorn brings to your relationship—including an independent and comfortable lifestyle. You will lead Capricorn to a greater self-image.

You're spontaneous and bubbly; Capricorn is more laidback, even solitary. As your relationship develops, this urge for privacy may become a pretty big stumbling block. Develop strong levels of intimacy and sexual honesty and you will overcome this problem. Even though Capricorn is traditional, you can break that trend and help them become more daring sexually.

Capricorns born between 23 December and 1 January are probably hard nuts to crack, but don't let this deter you from the challenge of bringing love to this traditional star sign.

You are most compatible with Capricorns born between 2 and 12 January, as they complement your strongly communicative nature. They may have issues about power and control, but you might just be able to communicate your way out of that and build a relationship that will satisfy you both. They are also quite open to exploring life with you.

Sex and love will be tied up with money and material security in a relationship with Capricorns born between 13 and 20 January. These Capricorns are lucky for you and are a little more philosophical, even though they are prudent with their expenses.

LIBRA + AQUARIUS

Air + Air = Wind

Aquarius is one of the most 'far out' signs and quite likely one of the most misunderstood. But this won't stop you from developing a great emotional and romantic connection with them. Aquarius is forward thinking, intellectual and somewhat similar to your own personality, only wilder and more wilful.

You're attracted to the spontaneous and witty character of this star sign and this stimulates every level of your being. You're likely to hit it off the moment you meet them and in some cases when air signs come together it can be love at first sight. Even if you don't want to go that far, you'll realise that there's probably something pretty special about your connection together.

Both of you are keenly interested in people—understanding them and serving them in some capacity. Both of you have a common interest in this sense and can work together towards some greater humanitarian ideal. This is a combination of the Libran understanding of human relationships and the Aquarian revolutionary spirit to improve the community and the world as a whole.

Being the diplomat, you'll be the partner who balances the relationship and stops it from spinning out of control. You have the ability to bring peace to the restless Aquarian spirit. They need you and the more they spend time with you the more they will realise this.

You love to spend time talking with each other and, no matter how much you learn about each other, there will still be more to be revealed. This is what keeps your relationship alive and exciting even if you've been in a long-term relationship together.

It's good to know that you both have unconventional views on love and marriage and you'll both be prepared to wait it out rather than diving into a traditional ceremony. Don't forget that Aquarius is a sign of free love and the new age, so what would you expect? They need to explore life before sending down their roots.

If you're looking for something really out of the ordinary in the way of love you can expect an electric romance with Aquarians born between 21 and 30 January. You will be completely infatuated; but please note: this partnership may not be destined to be a lifelong one. Enjoy it while it lasts.

Your best karmic combination would be with an Aquarian born between 31 January and 8 February. You have a great psychological connection with them and your romance will develop quite naturally. Expressing how you feel to each other will be the fuel that keeps a long-term relationship going.

In the different grades of Aquarius, those born between 9 and 19 February very closely resemble you in many ways as they are also partly ruled by Venus, your ruling planet. This can turn into a very special romance so there doesn't seem to be much that can get in the way of your love for each other on every level—emotionally, mentally and physically.

LIBRA + PISCES

Air + Water = Rain

The differences between Libra and Pisces are numerous. Libra, you're all head and Pisces is all heart. Pure heart. It's as simple as that. In other words, bridging the gap between you in this partnership will take some effort on both of your parts. Feeling versus intellect will always be the sticking point in love between you.

You'll either love each other completely or totally bamboozle each other. When I say Pisces is all heart I mean they are the most intuitive and spiritual of the zodiac signs and prefer to live an inner life, sometimes according to many, with their heads way up in the clouds. To your way of thinking as well, you may find them a little out of touch, maybe even off with the faeries. This won't stop you from loving them but they are not an easy character to understand.

Pisces prefer to operate from an intuitive level, relying on their instinctive responses rather than rationalising everything, like you do. You are a verbal communicator whereas Pisces transmits mysterious innuendoes and non-verbal signals.

Sometimes Pisces is completely disconnected from the world around them and this is because in their moments of reverie they are connected to a deeper, vaster source of love, which makes them unconditional in their approach to relationships. You might be overwhelmed by their capacity to love even though they may not communicate in ways you would expect. When you finally experience their tender, compassionate love they will win you over lock, stock and barrel.

Interestingly, Pisces enjoy socialising but more dispassionately than you. They are quite happy to let you take the lead in social circumstances while they observe the goings-on from 'cloud nine'. As long as they have their own private time and space to explore their own inner selves, they will be happy to share some of that time with you as well.

Sexually, Libra and Pisces will experience something quite unique due to their unconditional and pure love. Pisces can facilitate self-realisation for Libra both sexually and emotionally.

With Pisces born between 20 and 28 or 29 February, get ready for an unusual ride—these people are not normal. They may ultimately be too hard to deal with because they don't fit into your conceptual framework.

Pisceans born between 1 and 10 March will fit well with you professionally. You both have a business connection and these Pisces will work with you in ways that help you achieve your goals and meet your deadlines. This is probably more likely to be a financial or career-based relationship.

A great combination for you is with Pisces born between 11 and 20 March. These people touch your soul and bring you into contact with a loving part of your nature that you never knew existed. They are by far the most spiritual among the Piscean group and are destined to do something important in life. By being involved in a relationship with them you too will be part of this important mission.

LIBRA

2009: The Year Ahead

... for better or worse, our future will be determined in large part by our dreams and by the struggle to make them real.

—Mihaly Csikszentmihalyi

Romance and friendship

Pluto, the most distant planet in our solar system, has slowly and almost imperceptibly been working on your deeper self and slowly transforming you over recent months. Can you feel it? Your emotional life and therefore your personal interactions with friends and family members are undergoing a radical transformation during this cycle of your life. But this is no ordinary influence and great responsibility is placed upon you to manage your inner as well as your outer life in 2009.

Much of your focus in the first part of the year no doubt will be on your personal family affairs. In association with Pluto, the celestial bodies of Mars, the Sun, Jupiter and also Mercury create a powerhouse of energy that demands attention on your home front. You'll be actively engaged in dealing with many practical and personal issues in this arena. Mars and Sun in particular are hot and fiery planets, which may, if you let them, disrupt your peace of mind and day-to-day life affairs. If you let them!

Fortunately, Mercury and Jupiter afford you some balance in this respect and will in fact bless you with the ability to make peace and genuinely foster a spirit of understanding among all concerned. You have the ability to take your relationships to a new level simply through engaging in deeper and more meaningful discussions. Even if others happen to be aggressive in their approach, you will be able to keep a level head and create some important breakthroughs this year.

Several planets also influence the area of your horoscope dealing with children and youngsters in general. Much of your attention will be focused around them, especially if you're a parent. The loving combination of the Moon and Venus is an excellent omen, stimulating understanding, sensitivity and affection. Your relationships of a maternal or paternal nature will go well this year and a so-called a generation gap may evaporate.

This year's horoscope is also very promising for Libra in respect of romantic and sexual relationships. January and also February highlight your involvement with the opposite sex and the movement of Venus rapidly takes over in February when it hits on your zone of marriage. It does this only after making contact with the exciting and unpredictable Uranus. If you had any sense of planning or scheduling at this time it will more than likely go out the door as your head is spinning from some sort of romantic overload. However, you must choose your partners carefully. You are likely to be hot and impulsive and a few one-night stands at this time won't be out of the question.

A cluster of planets also invigorates your romantic and social zones in March. This sounds like a 'triple whammy' astrologically and, throughout the first quarter of 2009, you may have very little time to do anything other than manage your social agenda. Are you complaining? I hope not. You know the old saying, 'When it rains, it pours'? Well, this is one of those times.

Towards the end of March and April you may be feeling a little heavy in the heart and not at all as up-beat as in the previous months. Perhaps burning the candle at both ends is partly the reason for this and you'll need to take note of your body's signals to maximise your vitality. If you keep pushing yourself at this time, your health may suffer and, of course, you may not be able to fulfil some of those wonderful social obligations that as a Libran you naturally look forward to.

You may find the demands of your relationships a little hard to handle throughout April, even though your affection for your lover or spouse is strong and the feeling also mutual.

Venus moves into reverse motion, hinting at some unresolved issues in your marriage or most intimate relationship. You may need to go back through time to get at the heart of any unspoken difficulties you are experiencing. Your partner or spouse may be quiet, aloof and unresponsive. However, don't play the blame game during this cycle because doing so will only make matters worse.

With Saturn moving slowly through your zone of charitable works throughout most of 2009, you'll be spending a lot of time helping others and listening to their problems. You mustn't make this a habit because you may become just another addiction for them when it comes to pouring their problems onto you. Know where to draw the line between advice and showing others how to be responsible for their own life decisions and problem solving. Throughout May you will need to dedicate time to your friends and prove that friendship is not a superficial thing to you.

The conjunction of Venus and Mars is excellent for Libra throughout May as they traverse your marriage and then sexual zones in June. Venus also moves into its direct motion, indicating that the previous problems will not only be cleared up but your intimacy will be hotter than ever. During this time of the year I predict a great deal of physical and sexual satisfaction, which will reignite failing relationships.

In July, these physical and sexual impulses may reach a deeper level emotionally and even spiritually, resulting in some revelations for both you and your partner. If you've been married for some time, this could be the revival you've been longing for. Make hay while the sun shines.

Your sense of self is very powerful throughout August and, if you have felt a decline in self-confidence, you need not worry during this phase because your popularity will skyrocket. This will continue into September when your ruling planet Venus transits your most important social zone. With the added influence of Jupiter and Neptune, some of your social ideals will reach a pinnacle and your popularity will further increase with umpteen offers and invitations to parties, gatherings and other club or social activities.

Friends will be important at this time, but you may also feel a sense of humanitarianism resulting in a connection with someone, or a group of people, who may introduce you to charitable activities through which you find a new sense of inner satisfaction. This also indicates a recommencement of some previous hobby or interest that you may have mothballed for a few years. You'll come back with a great creative energy and produce some wonderful works of art or handicraft, if this is your cup of tea. Around this same time, the Sun and Saturn cause you to remain indoors and this is probably just as well given your desire to delve into these creative and humanitarian realms.

Health issues and assistance rendered to older, frailer relatives will take centre stage throughout October. You may have to deal with the finances and day-to-day aspects of an ageing parent's life. This may be difficult and you will be confronted by certain philosophical issues. If you do so in a non-judgemental manner, with the sense of surrendering to life's challenges, you'll come out of this an even better person.

Saturn makes a very important transition on the 30th of October. Moving to your Sun sign, it ushers in a new two-and-a-half-year cycle, which, for most other star signs, can be viewed with some apprehension. Not so for you, Libra, because Saturn is most comfortable in your star sign. Certainly, a combination of the Sun and Saturn causes you to take a more serious view of things over the coming years, but this needn't be a bad thing. You'll finally realise that it is time to weed out those elements of your life that have been holding you back; people who have not reciprocated in the game of love. This therefore seems to me to be a period of increased self-respect and spiritual awareness for you.

You may become so aware of many things that have previously slipped past your attention in your social and romantic lives. It's as if a floodlight will shine upon many of your relationships with the result that you'll want to change and even remove some of them from your life. The last two months of the year will be important in deciding who stays and who goes. Some of these decisions may not be easy but you will realise that at different times in your life you outgrow people just like you outgrow certain fashions or passing fads.

As the year comes to a close, some may even regard you as ruthless for the change that they will see in you. You mustn't look back, however, because life is a series of changes and you will realise most importantly that for growth to occur you have to let go of certain things. Jupiter and Neptune will continue to raise your personal standards, which means you are likely to find yourself in the company of a whole new batch of people who have much more to offer you. This seems like a great way to finish the year and to glide into 2010.

Work and money

Your mental responses are lightning fast this year and will be one of your greatest assets professionally. At the same time, this could create some instability for you because you'll be a little bored with the routine of your work and this might push you into exploring any new opportunities that come your way. Your expressions will be free and progressive and you won't allow anyone to push you around, even if you're not in a position of authority.

In January and February your independence will continue to grow and your desire to back traditional systems could cause you some sudden run-ins with employers if you're not careful. A lunar eclipse on the 10th of February is telling, particularly on your finances, and this will herald the beginning of a reappraisal of your attitude to money. This could be a turning point for many Librans this year.

Your desire to take a punt and explore uncharted territory will be notable around March when Jupiter, Mercury, Mars and Neptune fire up your fifth zone of speculation. If you aren't doing anything creative then you'll certainly make sure that also changes. You're wired for excitement this year in your work and no one's going to stop you. You have a strong desire to transform everything about your career and this year the sign of Libra is detaching itself from anything that is holding you back from achieving the best.

This year you realise you have talents that have been submerged for a long time and you can bring these to the fore in April when Mars and Uranus, the progressive planet, bring renewed vitality to your workplace and work systems. You will want to implement a whole swag of techniques that can make your life more efficient. This is also a very original influence upon you and you will be apt to come up with novel and inventive techniques for making your work not only groundbreaking but a lot of fun as well.

Some of these influences are in contradiction due to the fact that Mercury commences the year in the very practical sign of Capricorn. This sets the trend and sets it positively, I might say, for you to balance much of this very way-out behaviour with a realistic and cautious element as well. You can use the power of Mercury to organise your circumstances and prove your leadership. Studying concrete subjects that extend beyond the specific aspects of your work skills into human relations and how to improve your co-worker relationships will also prove to be of interest to you and will certainly create a turn for the better.

In April and May your self-discipline will be quite strong but you will also prove to be popular with the public, making some great contacts to further your ambitions at this time. Your passion and enthusiasm will be infectious and you're likely to win over several allies, whose ideas you can convert into ready cash. You will want to use your instinctive sales ability.

Real estate is also an area that you're likely to be successful in this year. You don't necessarily have to work in this industry to realise some substantial profits. Legal matters and documentation surrounding such issues, which can bogged down throughout May, are likely to improve after July when Mercury enters your tenth zone of professional esteem. If you haven't yet been able to prove your worth to the bank, July and August could be a time where your bank balance looks much healthier and your home loan will be easier to attain.

Take care not to be too reactive in your personal or business financial partnerships. Disagreements may occur during this period due to Venus and Mars associating in your zone of shared resources. Utilising your human resources and communication skills will be useful in making sure these financial differences don't overtake the relationships.

Your popularity is strong from August, with Venus reaching the zenith of your horoscope. You'll make a great impact; not only on your clients, co-workers and friends, but on your employers and other important people who can help bolster your professional standing. Your ego may be fairly strong at this time, but harmlessly so, I might say.

Venus, Mercury and Saturn entering your zone of secrets in October hint at the fact that you may need a little time out to re-establish the direction you wish to travel. This is a good policy if you've been overworked and need time to collect your energies. You'll come out of this period in November much more refreshed and, with Saturn also making an important transition to your Sun sign, you'll be more focused, disciplined and ready to do the hard yards to achieve even greater successes throughout the coming year.

Journeys and interesting new communications in December ensure that the last month of the year is also jam-packed with excitement and positive omens for your professional success.

Karma, luck and meditation

Home is where the heart is and this year some of your most satisfying moments will be found within the four walls of your own residence. Your spiritual awareness doesn't need others to enlighten you. Contemplative practices are best done without the distraction of too many people pulling you here, there and everywhere.

January, February, April and May prove to be satisfying months from a psychological and spiritual perspective. Mercury, your planet of higher knowledge, reveals insights that are intellectual and practical and will be used to improve your luck. During this time yoga classes and other meditative practices will come easily to you. If in the past self-study has been hard, it will be child's play this year.

April and May are wonderful months for you romantically as Venus brings with it renewed optimism in your relationships. Venus is your ruling planet and also controls your self-transformation. It is through your relationships that these parts of your personality will move to a new level and help you actualise your true potential. You will raise the standard and expect so much more from others, too. Your good fortune this year comes from fostering mutually supportive relationships.

On the worldly level, luck is strong for you in August and this again is due to Venus. New pathways will open up to you. At this time the world will be your oyster but be prepared to take on the responsibilities that come with this added luck.

The transition of Saturn to your Sun sign early in November till the end of the year will reflect that Lady Luck doesn't support you without some degree of obligation. If you're able to come to terms with this important karmic lesson, you'll be all the richer for your experiences in the coming year.

LIBRA

2009: Month by Month Predictions

Pessimism is a very easy way out when you're considering what life really is, because pessimism is a short view of life ... If you take a long view, I do not see how you can be pessimistic about the future of man or the future of the world.

—Robertson Davies

Highlights of the month

Many of your personal desires will be fulfilled in the first part of the year due to the full Moon in your zone of accomplishment. Up to the 11th your social life is busy but this will be only against the backdrop of a strong focus on family affairs. You'll choose to entertain at home and bring family and friends together at home.

The 13th to the 15th causes you to be serious due to the Moon's association with Saturn. This is okay because we all need a balance against too much excessive socialising. It will get you back on an even keel. Around the 12th, when Mercury goes retrograde, confusing family matters need to be dealt with. Promises are broken and you may lose faith in someone you had previously trusted.

This month is important for your love affairs, which will be high on your agenda. This is due to Venus being in your love zone with the Moon and Neptune. You are dreamy, passionate and idealistic about what you want from your relationships. It could go one of two ways: either you will meet someone who is just perfect and who fits your ideal image; or, conversely, you will be severely disappointed to find that the person of your dreams is only human after all. Be realistic between the 15th and the 17th.

On the 18th, use your dynamic energy to improve things, not to create disputes. You'll be sure of your own mind but will not be able to convince someone else of your argument. This could get out of hand and make family life unbearable. Sweeten the truth if you must tell it as it is.

On the 20th and 21st you can expect a considerable amount of travelling, probably due to renovations and other home affairs. Make sure you have your list with you as you may get to your destination only to find you've forgotten something necessary for the job.

Your work and professional activities are much more focused after the 24th when Mars and Saturn are in favourable relationship. Although you may not be driven to achieve a lot this month, you can still do preliminary work behind the scenes.

The solar eclipse on the 26th is an important phenomenon and takes place in your zone of love affairs, children and creativity. Pay special attention to these areas of your life at this time because these planetary events usually herald important revelations. Secrets could be revealed and may make or break a relationship.

Watch your health around the 28th as nervousness makes you accident prone. The 30th is better for relationships, which are much easier.

Romance and friendship

On the 3rd try not to impose your values on a friend today because this could spell trouble. You may have to grin and bear the behaviour of someone in your peer group, if only to keep the peace. Under no circumstances enter into power plays as you'll only be giving satisfaction to the other person by losing your self-composure.

Poor health between the 5th and the 8th is the result of too much effort and not enough fun. You need to take the pressure off by enjoying yourself in your line of work. There's no point putting in the hours trying to prove you're a superman or superwoman if it's undermining your wellbeing.

The comments of a close friend or perhaps even a stranger will inspire and invigorate you on the 11th. It's nice to know that you're still wanted and can make an impact on others, even if you haven't felt exactly on top of your game recently. Your general level of energy should improve between the 12th and the 16th. With the exception of the 14th, this should be an uplifting period.

You may be premature in choosing to run away by taking a holiday on the 20th or 21st. Do your homework, investigate the possibilities and, of course, make sure your finances are capable of handling the vision you have in mind. More importantly, take note of your motivation because escapism won't provide you the pleasure you seek.

You mustn't try too hard in the romance area of your life between the 26th and 30th because desperation is the last thing a prospective lover is attracted to. On the other hand, this is a creative time and should give you considerable satisfaction a long as you associate with people of a like mind.

Work and money

Are you trying to keep up with friends in the Lifestyle Department? This is not a good idea; in fact, it's a recipe for depression if they keep one-upping you. Being content in the circumstances you happen to be in is your challenge between the 8th and 14th. This attitude of mind will bring you more happiness than the designer label outfit a friend is wearing.

I see considerable enjoyment away from your usual social–work group between the 18th and the 22nd. You'll be surprised at how much pleasure you can derive from staying indoors and working quietly without the disturbance of your usual office noises.

Some confusion surrounding a statement made on the 25th shouldn't bother you until you hear the full story. If you're relying on hearsay and third-party interpretations, this could create problems for you in the workplace. Get the full story from the horse's mouth.

You discover something that will be useful in your financial dealings on the 30th. It may be a delicate balancing act to get all your affairs in order but, with the right attitude and advice, you will come out the winner and with your finances getting stronger.

Destiny dates

Positive: 1, 2, 4, 19, 24

Negative: 17

Mixed: 3, 5, 6, 7, 8, 9, 10, 11, 12, 13, 14, 15, 16, 20, 21, 25, 26, 27, 28, 29, 30

Highlights of the month

Family affairs are back on track on the 1st when Mercury moves back into forward motion. A decision is finally reached that benefits all concerned. Tempers are appeased and cordial relations return to normal, especially with children. Between the 3rd and the 8th a greater understanding between your relatives is achieved. Leading up to the 10th you will still feel concerned about a child who may not be communicating their feelings. Don't force the hand as this will sort itself out in due course.

Your work and the way your health is affected by your daily schedule are highlighted between the 11th and the 13th. It may be that getting up earlier to do those extra chores will make you feel better rather than leaving them till the midnight hours. You'll also find yourself back at the gym if you've slackened off a little and this is a great time to knock off a few of those extra pounds and get back into shape. This will reduce your stress levels and make you more efficient at work.

After the 15th, managing your partner's debts will require serious discussions to talk sense into them. Your values will be at odds so think of clever ways to help them curb their expenses. You will be exasperated by the 19th because your words are falling on deaf ears.

Apart from finances, the excellent news is that Venus enters your marriage sector. Of course, if you're already attached to someone this will not impact upon you as strongly but it still means your love life will experience much more sizzle at this time, particularly between the 22nd and the 26th. It also has a beneficial influence on any of your negotiations and makes you popular on the business scene.

The new Moon on the 25th offers a few Librans another shot at a job opportunity that may have fallen through previously. You might have thought you'd lost a position only to find now that the vacancy arises once again. It's time to make contact with recruitment officers and employment agencies to throw your hat in the ring because an unexpected turn of event works in your favour. You'll be successful in any competitive arena.

On the 27th and 28th you will have to manage the excessive stress levels of a co-worker but the situation will be more comical than tragic in your view. You may have to stop yourself from laughing but try to remind yourself that what appears amusing to you may be dead serious to another. A little humour can sometimes lighten the state of affairs but make sure your timing is impeccable or you could end up demoralising the other person.

Romance and friendship

You needn't struggle with your identity on the 5th even if you're in the company of people who have become quite successful. You may not feel quite up to their standard and, even if they are judging you for not being as good as them, you'll realise it's all in your head and actually not the case at all. Don't be too hard on yourself and simply be yourself.

Your social environment is a mixed bag between the 7th and the 10th. Some of your friends could be downright irritating.

You need to find a quiet corner in a cafe with your best mate to shut out the world. It may not be altogether possible at first, but everyone will soon get the idea if you are consistent in your demands.

You can shine among your peers and make a bold statement about who you are on the 13th. You have the attention of those who count so what you say and do over the coming days will propel you forward in a big way.

You'll feel really happy in your relationships between the 16th and the 23rd. With the Sun spotlighting love affairs this month you are excited about the long-term prospects. Your social agenda will be jam-packed from the 25th of the full Moon to the 27th. You will enjoy each other's company in greater measure than you have for a long time.

You will be disappointed by the actions of a friend on the 28th. This could be associated with money and wasn't intended to hurt you in any way. If your ego gets in the road, you will no doubt be taking this matter far too personally. It's best to let this slide so it doesn't interfere with what is otherwise a pretty good relationship.

Work and money

Was it $50 or $100 that you loaned him (or was it they who loaned you the money)? What a confused state of affairs on the 2nd! Unless you start keeping accurate records for your transactions you'll find yourself in a state of financial upheaval. It's time to change that.

You'll be creatively dry, professionally speaking, from the 6th till the 9th, but take heart because this is only temporary and things will improve. Someone will cramp your style and feels you are better than them at what you do. Envy is a tough one to deal with but this is what will challenge you at this time.

The burden of a co-worker can be lessened by effective planning on your part on the 13th. There's no point complaining that you don't have the time or resources to do what is necessary to help them. Think outside the square and utilise your time more efficiently to satisfy all concerned, especially by the 19th.

A child or younger person you are associated with could be spinning out of control and this will affect your professional obligations on the 23rd. Lead by example and don't argue. Actions always speak louder than words.

Destiny dates

Positive: 1, 3, 4, 6, 11, 12, 13, 16, 17, 18, 20, 21, 22, 24, 25, 26

Negative: 2, 9, 15

Mixed: 5, 7, 8, 10, 19, 23, 27, 28

Highlights of the month

Venus continues to cruise in one of the most important love zones of your horoscope, spotlighting your interest in romance and public relations. Your discussions will be feisty, especially on the 2nd, but by the 5th what seemed certain to you will start to become more nebulous.

This is also highlighted on the 7th when Venus moves retrograde and causes you to rethink a romantic situation. This is not a bad idea because it always prudent to take a second look at your relationships, especially if they're fresh off the assembly line of life. It's easy to get caught up in the excitement of something new, isn't it?

You generally have a better sense of yourself, as shown by the full Moon on the 11th. You'll be emotionally expressive, wanting to give much of yourself to your friends and others generally. Expect a few swinging moods, however, as the Moon is notorious for making you feel like a pendulum, especially when it is very bright.

Your work practices could get out of hand by the 15th when Mars brings out the workaholism within your nature. You'll find yourself taking on additional chores both at work and at home only to find yourself being run into the ground. The odd thing about this is that there may be no external pressure on you and this is something you bring upon yourself. Be kind yourself as there's no rush or deadline making you behave this way. Mars creates digestive disturbances, so take care with your food and don't eat on the run. Rather, you should savour your food—each and every morsel.

Between the 20th and 24th you will feel a lull in your self-confidence probably by being outshone by someone in your group. Rather than withdrawing into your shell like a tortoise, why not raise the benchmark and improve your skills? This could be the catalyst you've been waiting for to push you towards greater professional excellence.

Some miscommunication around the 27th points out some of the problems that occur when you are doing too much and don't pay attention to the detail. This could be like sending an e-mail to the wrong person and then embarrassingly having to explain yourself. God forbid that someone gets hold of a discussion you're having about them to a third party. Double-check all your e-mails with this in mind before pressing the 'send' button.

On the 30th and 31st the combination of the Sun and Venus will put you in the right place at the right time. This is particularly lucky for you if you happen to be out there looking for Mr or Ms Right. This planetary combination is a well-known power for drawing romance to you.

Romance and friendship

You could have some problems with women at home or socially on the 4th. Keep a cool head. You'll be surprised but diplomacy will work to secure more respect.

On the 7th and 8th it's a balance between sensitivity, sentimentality and straight up-and-down facts when you are dealing with friends. If you let your emotions intrude on your conversations, others will see you as a pushover. Be quietly assertive in the way you speak.

You mustn't let a friend dictate the course of events on the 11th. They will be confused and erratic in their lives and will cause the same in yours if you allow it. You need to run the show your way—not theirs. Be strong and demand what you want from your peers.

Your mind is flighty and making a decision between the 16th and the 21st will be extremely difficult. You'll see both sides of a situation and will swing from one viewpoint to another. If you can't make up your mind, ask the advice of a close friend who will have the solution.

If you can't be consistent in your emotional life between the 24th and the 28th, it's best to bow out for a while then return to the relationship when you feel refreshed. It could be one of those times when intimacy is not at its peak and attempting to do as much as possible will only be a waste of your time and others'.

Your lover or spouse is unusually demanding on the 30th, but try to see beneath the surface of what is motivating their behaviour. Are they feeling a little unloved due to your busy schedule? It takes only a little time to reassure them that everything is fine from your end of the relationship. Try it.

Work and money

A job offer opportunity appears out of nowhere around the 6th and gives you the chance to revive your self-confidence. Your responses will be as swift so take the precautions you need to investigate the offer calmly and practically.

You will experience new friendships that help you develop ideas for an independent and exciting business. Share your ideas, especially between the 11th and the 16th.

Put on a new outfit and look a million bucks on the 22nd. Raise your standard to let others see how professional and successful you are, even if you haven't yet reached the level you'd like. Success breeds success.

If you're house hunting, and the going has been tough, you might find something that is just in keeping with your lifestyle needs around the new Moon of the 26th. On the motor vehicle front, you may also need to splurge on a car service or something to at least maintain its value.

A sudden inclination to throw away a large sum of money on the 29th will give you instant gratification but delayed regret. It's not advisable to use plastic for purchases. Term payments would be a better idea to stay on top of your cash flow.

Destiny dates

Positive: 2, 3, 5, 6, 12, 13, 14

Negative: 23, 31

Mixed: 4, 7, 8, 11, 16, 17, 18, 19, 20, 21, 22, 24, 25, 26, 27, 28, 29, 30

Highlights of the month

Transformations in your family continue and in an even bigger and better way due to the motion of Pluto. There may be secrets now emerging, influences from your early life, which are noticeably affecting your personal and most intimate relationships. Hidden feelings and other unspoken thoughts may come to the surface during April and help clear the air to make life more comfortable for you in all of your relationships, not just those from your historical family. This is particularly highlighted around the 4th.

If you've been unable to address these important issues, Mercury's movement to your zone of deeper emotional issues on the 10th help all parties to clear the air and allow the dust to settle. Because this has to do with shared resources, joint money and savings, you may have been biting your tongue and not been courageous enough to put your foot down on the manner in which your money has been handled.

If you're married and have a joint bank account from which funds are being used to pay the bills, you will be feeling as if there is some inequity in the way the money is being spent. Your partner will in fact be more amenable to hearing your side of the story, so don't freak out.

Your willpower becomes much more potent between the 23rd and the 25th. Your leadership qualities are waxing and this is the perfect time to assert yourself in your place of employment, especially if others are not pulling their weight and you have been doing more than your fair share of the work. You can align yourself with one of your managers or senior co-workers to create a better reputation for yourself during this time interval.

Mercury and Neptune cause fuzzy headedness between the 26th and the 29th, so your decisions should be postponed for a few days until you are in full possession of the facts that are required to make an important decision. This is important because to maintain your integrity you'll need to be seen to be consistent in the way you execute your responsibilities. Don't be distracted by any hard luck story at this time because you may find it difficult to regain your focus.

Many of the transformative influences I have been speaking to you about with respect to your family and domestic situation this year will now also be manifest in your professional life. Pluto is again responsible for this and can help you make the appropriate changes you secretly desire deep within you. On the 30th your ambitions are very powerful and you may have now reached a point where your creative visualisation and your wilful intention come together to help you achieve something quite extraordinary.

Romance and friendship

You've reached the top of the mountain in some aspect of your life and will reconsider your life plan between the 8th and the 15th. If you're currently in a relationship, your partner will fully support your decision and this will give you more confidence in moving forward. You will need to change your social plan slightly to fit in with this strategy.

If you're afraid of showing a little more sensitivity in your love life it's because you think others are going to take advantage. You may be absolutely right on the 20th and 21st! Pick your mark before wearing your heart on your sleeve. They may take delight in your hardship and use that against you.

This is a good phase because Venus, your ruling planet, is in your marriage zone. With Mercury also creating favourable luck for you from the 22nd to the 25th, you should be feeling on top of the world. During this cycle almost everything you do will be successful. A social engagement now will also lift your spirits.

A change is as good as a holiday and on the 27th your mind will be contemplating the possibilities of a journey. To gain the maximum out of this cycle, stay away from friends and other mental or social distractions. You'll come to a decision more easily. You mustn't be afraid to taking time away on your own. Part of the exploratory process is to discover aspects of yourself, not just the world.

An obligation has to be met on the 29th but enjoy the process rather than begrudging the time or money you have to invest. A luxurious period is now pending with some new outfits and other long-desired artefacts being acquired on one of those shopping sprees most of us only dream about.

Work and money

Your work will receive a lift and you're relieved of some of the pressures between the 2nd and the 5th. There will be more socialising involved in your work practices and a new friendship, possibly even romance, arises out of this.

You mustn't postpone important legal or bureaucratic documents on the 9th, as cumbersome and time-consuming as they may be. You may have overlooked additional costs associated with a deadline. Put aside time to get your dirty work out of the way.

You may have been loaned something that gave you a slightly better lifestyle and a taste of that experience will cause you to try harder to make that a permanent feature of your life. With your desires come financial requirements and the need for more work and responsibility. Are you up to it? You'll be focused on these issues around the 20th.

You will learn something that will be an eye-opener between the 24th and the 26th. If you've turned away from a specific topic you'll find that a friend reintroduces you to it. This is also a perfect time to enrol in courses or a study group, which will help to improve your skills in the work place.

Destiny dates

Positive: 2, 3, 4, 5, 8, 10, 11, 12, 13, 14, 15, 22, 23, 24, 25, 30

Negative: 21, 28, 29

Mixed: 9, 20, 26, 27

Highlights of the month

You'll have no problem keeping the passionate flames of romance burning brightly throughout the month of May. You can thank Venus and Mars for this as they combine in your most prominent zone of romance and personal relationships.

In close proximity the planet Uranus causes even more excitement and so I can safely predict that May will be quite memorable for you, whether single or attached. On the 5th and 6th, these energies will be very pronounced and you should make sure you are not otherwise occupied because this will only result in frustration. Be available when that new date comes knocking on your door or makes a telephone call.

This month you can also catch up with long-forgotten friends due to the movement of the Moon with the past karma points of your horoscope. This can be scary, especially if fifteen or twenty years has elapsed since last seeing these people, but you mustn't let the concept of age ruffle you. Between the 10th and the 16th enjoy old friends and reminisce old times as it will be thoroughly pleasurable for you.

The 17th and 18th I caution you to take care with your health and in particular not to let monetary pressures get you down. Write a plan, set a target for how you're going to pay off your outstanding debts and credit cards, because this could be eating away at you and undermining your vitality. You probably hate the word budget but this is an excellent way to rein in your spending and gain peace of mind.

Love and intimacy will take centre stage between the 19th and the 23rd as the Moon combines with passionate Venus and Mars. You can fall in love all over again if you're married and realise that there's still more to learn about your partner. Singles, don't be too quick off the mark because your good taste could cause regrets after sultry and inebriating evenings. One-night stands will be appealing.

The new Moon on the 24th together with Mercury makes travel very appealing and there's every chance you will decide to pack your bags in a moment's notice and head for the hills. Finding peace and solace within could be the motivating factor behind such trips, even short ones, because you'll be seeking spiritual guidance under these transits. You may even meet someone who acts as a spiritual adviser and points out the proper direction for you, philosophically speaking.

For Librans staying home and not venturing out, work and professional pursuits are spotlighted from the 26th to the 29th. Some of your long-forgotten friends mentioned above may also somehow be entwined in your work activities.

Romance and friendship

Your romantic feelings are powerful throughout the first part of the month, particularly up until the 15th. I only hope you have someone with whom you can share your deep emotions. If you're currently in a relationship, the feeling will be particularly mutual as the month progresses. It may be a good idea to set aside some time for a quiet candlelight dinner and some cuddles.

You may even receive a gift, especially around the 19th. Mars and Venus also increase the temperature, sexually speaking.

Your interest in literature, language and speaking will increase under this same planetary cycle. I'm not suggesting you'll become Shakespeare, but you will begin to understand the power of words and how this can shape people's opinion of you.

Pay special attention to the way conversations develop in your social arena between the 20th and the 24th because this can bring you an unexpected chance for new friendships.

Another journey is on the cards after the 25th and this will give you the opportunity to kill two or maybe even three birds with one stone. Plan your agenda and your schedule a little more carefully so that you can take advantage of some free time, which will be made available to you through this additional chore. A telephone conversation you have around this time will also make you feel happy.

Your insights on the 29th and 30th are a little too close to the bone and someone might retaliate as a result. Yes, what you're saying is certainly the truth, but you have to share your truth in a way that doesn't ruffle their feathers if they are overly sensitive. You could find yourself back-pedalling to try to explain how this wasn't a personal attack on them.

Work and money

You have financial differences with business partners and accountants around the 3rd. In any case there is some confusion over tax or other banking issues and these may also pop up later in the month. Don't jump to conclusions and beat anyone over the head until you've heard their side of the story. It's quite likely you've overlooked some of your own spending and once the bottom line is explained to you it will all make sense.

Remain alert to the possibility of new promotional opportunities between the 7th and the full Moon of the 9th. You might hear something on the grapevine that you would ordinarily discard or consider as useless gossip. This time there may be some truth to it and a window of opportunity grants you access to a brighter pathway in your life. Jump at any new opportunity.

Stay on top of your spending habits between the 17th to the 23rd because your generosity will catch up with you. One round of drinks becomes five, then ten, and before you know it you're a dipping into your credit card to pay for your everyday expenses. Be moderate so that your finances don't suffer.

Destiny dates

Positive: 5, 6, 7, 9, 10, 11, 12, 13, 14, 15, 16, 24, 25, 26, 27, 28

Negative: 3, 29, 30

Mixed: 17, 18, 19, 20, 21, 22, 23

Highlights of the month

Your actions will be unbridled this month so I caution you against dangerous activities, even sports that you normally feel are safe for you. Throughout June, Mars transits the dangerous segment of your horoscope, which is why I ask you to take extra physical precautions.

On the second, and the full Moon of the 7th, don't travel if you feel particularly stressed. Better still, get someone else to drive and of course if you happen to be attending a function where you are drinking, take a taxi if you can't get a lift from someone else.

Higher education is spotlighted as the Sun triggers your curiosity for wisdom and extended knowledge. Book yourself into a study or discussion group or perhaps a home-based correspondence course to hone your skills and expand your mind. The month of June is an excellent time to lift yourself to a new academic level.

You may have felt a little inadequate in some of your social engagements and these planetary transits give you the opportunity to make yourself more interesting, as well as offering you a better edge in the employment stakes. There may be one person in particular with whom you feel nervous due to their intellectual superiority. You can now put an end to that. Between the 8th and the 13th you'll be actively engaged in seeking the right type of subjects for your mind.

On the topic of education, Librans parents will need to strategise carefully their children's educational needs. You may be at odds with what your children feel is in their best interests. There could be significant changes from one school to another and the associated bureaucratic paperwork that goes with that. And, of course, don't forget the interviews with principals and teachers to make sure that these people will offer the best not only academically but ethically.

The new Moon on the 22nd will provide new insights into your life path. I mentioned that in the previous months you may have taken an interest in higher knowledge and meditative practices. Far from being intellectual exercises, you will truly feel the benefits and practically apply what you've been learning. Some of your friends might find you a little wacky but that won't bother you because peace of mind is the only criteria by which one should measure success—even material success.

You gain an advantage this month due to the Sun's magnificent placement in your career zone. This emphasises your popularity for a job well done. Some Librans will receive accolades and no doubt the financial rewards are soon to follow. Accepting an honour or simply moving into a better position via a promotion, are the possibilities for you as this month draws to a close.

Romance and friendship

If you get caught in the habit of rehashing the past, your relationship is bound to get bogged down, particularly around the 3rd and 4th. If you're having a disagreement or trying to resolve some issue with a friend or lover, it's imperative that you stick to the present facts and not move backwards in time. There may also be a problem of the discussion becoming way too personal. Again, keep your ego out of this and stick to the issue.

You are able to think much more deeply about your emotional needs under the planetary transits of the 11th to the 16th. If you've been surrounding yourself with people who are shallow, unimaginative and routine by nature, you will definitely be looking further a field to expand your personal self and your life generally. The moment you make this decision, you'll see a whole new circle of friends emerging.

You have a desire to get away from your normal domestic routine and I suggest that this it will be good for you sometime around the 17th or 18th. Variety is the spice of life. A change is as good as a holiday. Don't let anyone tell you otherwise. If a chance arises to house sit, you may seriously want to consider the offer on the 22nd, even if it is not something that will last long. The break will do you good.

You'll probably prefer to stay in rather than party or involve yourself with too many social activities between the 26th and the 28th. There's comfort with family, relatives and friends in the security of your own castle. You can revamp your living quarters around the 25th and purchasing that glossy interior design magazine might be something that will stimulate your creative energies.

Work and money

You need a strategy between the 6th and the 11th and, although you are normally good at this, your plan may come apart at the seams. Gather up your resources and reconnect with those people who can actually make things happen for you. This can happen around the 14th. If you've been doing everything yourself, delegation will be your key word. Surround yourself with people who will make the difference.

The period of the 16th to the 22nd will be extremely busy so be prepared or you will stress out. Be a step ahead of your co-workers who will have you picking up their loose ends because they don't have time to complete their own tasks. Let them know just how busy you are before each day starts.

Good fortune arrives from the least-expected areas in your life on the 23rd. A friend has news that can be exciting but also a little daunting on the 25th. You'll realise that to make something happen you have to have a plan and invest time and possibly money as well. It doesn't matter. If you're prepared to put in the time and goodwill, success is just around the corner.

Destiny dates

Positive: 2, 7, 12, 13, 14, 15, 23, 25, 26, 27, 28

Negative: 3, 4, 6, 7, 19, 20, 21

Mixed: 8, 9, 10, 11, 16, 17, 18, 22

Highlights of the month

July will prove to be a most important month in terms of your professional life. If you are a stay-at-home mum, your career too as a home-maker will also undergo some radical changes. Please note that the period of the 4th to the 6th is a time when your head will be much clearer and your judgement more sound.

Professional meetings throughout this period will be a good idea due to the lucky vibrations of the planets. If you don't actually work for a company or business you will have some concrete plans that you implement this month. There is an indication that a superior or someone with more experience will come to your assistance and help short cut your journey to success.

Any temporary blockage you feel this month is likely to clear up after the 8th. You will be challenged because it's the nature of the world to cut down tall poppies, isn't it? Success is a difficult thing for some people to handle, especially when it's another person's success (namely yours) they are dealing with. Your popularity continues to grow and you may end up becoming a favourite of your employer, much to the envy of others.

You may have to spend some time alone after the movement of Venus to your the ninth zone of long journeys. Your spouse or partner may have to travel and this may be related to business or just a long-overdue holiday to them. Don't mope about because you'll find that after a day or two you'll really enjoy your own space and will even find it hard to adjust when they return. Expect these circumstances to occur sometime around the 18th.

Some of your friends will leave you stone cold between the 20th and the 25th. They will be playing mind games with you and that's not your cup of tea. You'll be more interested in carving out a whole new niche of friendships. You may meet someone who is an unusual character and may be introduced by a third party by way of a blind date. This may be nerve wracking at first but you'll perform well and even make a long-term friendship with them.

I see you connecting with a new organisation, club or affiliation because you have so much to contribute at this time. Your creative and communal spirit is strong and therefore your offerings will be warmly received. If you are in a possessive relationship, however, your partner will find themselves envious and unable to accept your newfound independence. Between the 26th on the 30th you will have to spend considerable time justifying your behaviour.

Romance and friendship

Relationships are hot and exciting on the 4th, 6th, 7th, 8th and 9th and you have the chance to take your relationship to the next level. A third-party introduction could turn out better than you expect with Venus and Mars still giving you a dose of sexual confidence, particularly around the 13th and 14th. Dress to kill, not to appease the status quo or people around you. It's time to make a statement especially if you've been feeling like a wallflower for some time.

You have some strong intuitive hunches on the 15th and, if you meet someone with whom you feel uncomfortable, you should act upon these feelings. Don't be drawn into their glamorous story, especially if someone is asking you to part with your money. It's likely you won't see your money again and will kick yourself for not trusting your first impressions.

A friend will want to dominate the social landscape and you will certainly have difficulties trying to be diplomatic with them between the 20th and the 22nd. The alternative is that there is strength in numbers. If this individual is reminded that their behaviour is not acceptable—not just by you but by several people—there is a greater chance that they will see the error of their ways and start toeing the line once again. Democracy rules, remember?

Your energies are low after the 24th and you need to give yourself a break to recover. There will be too many people or circumstances crowding in on you and you haven't given yourself sufficient 'me' time. Get away from the rat race and re-establish your schedule in a peaceful and uplifting atmosphere. You will see things more clearly by the 27th and can make some firm decisions as a consequence.

Work and money

Performing work or service is easy from the 11th and you'll find yourself full of gusto and clarity. Strike while the iron is hot, make your mark and go for your dreams. There may be an opportunity awaiting you by the 17th, but you mustn't waste time because the competition is strong even if you are in a position to secure that promotion.

If you're not earning as much as the person next to you, even though they are probably doing exactly the same type of work, you need to ask questions of yourself, especially between the 20th and the 23rd. What can you do better, rather than how much more can you do? It's a matter of quality not quantity. Don't cast a judgement until you get a third person's opinion on things.

Keep an eye on your money or you will forget what you've done with it around the 24th. In the heat of the moment you will spend more than you are aware of only to find later that you haven't kept tabs on your expenditure. On the 25th you may also misplace valuables. Pay attention to what you're doing. That's the secret of not losing things.

Destiny dates

Positive: 4, 5, 6, 7, 8, 9, 11, 17

Negative: 15, 18, 26, 27, 28, 29, 30

Mixed: 20, 21, 22, 23, 24, 25

AUGUST

Highlights of the month

You mustn't overstep the bounds of good taste even if you're enthusiastic about your belief systems. Some of your friends will feel that you're trying to shove your opinions down their throats. Between the 2nd and 4th this may extend to relatives. If you have an opinion about the way something should be done and they don't agree this could create turmoil for you. Try to accept that others have their own way of doing things.

Mercury moves to the quiet part of your horoscope. It's an opportunity to you to catch up on correspondence, reflective thinking and planning. If busy either at home or in the workplace it requires creative manoeuvring on your part to give you free time. Between the 3rd and the 6th, spring cleaning of sorts may take place, but not of a worldly type.

This is a time of resolutions and weeding out those parts of your personality that are not serving you anymore. Be honest with yourself, especially around the 4th when what you discover about yourself will not be pleasant. It's the beginning of a distinct inner change for you. This is also highlighted by the lunar eclipse on the 6th, which is important for signifying major changes in our lives.

Between the 7th and the 12th, others' zest for you will give you a feeling of gratitude for the way your life is panning out. Your success will not be related to any financial benefits, just simply an inner satisfaction of happiness and contentment.

From the 15th it's 'all systems go' with work demanding more and more of you because of your ability to get the job done. You can't expect not to be wanted if you continue to perform at an optimum level and also look great, I might add! With Venus cruising through the upper part of your horoscope in August, you will be chosen to spearhead a new initiative because it's obvious that clients and business associates want to negotiate with you.

Creative Librans who have struggled to achieve fame may do so during the period of the 20th to the 30th when their ruling planet is at its strongest. Don't be shy in coming forward with your works of art, musical compositions or other handy crafts and expressions. You are better than you think.

Someone may recognise your talent and, if you don't have the assets to hold a public viewing of your work, you can always share the occasion quietly with some friends around and do it in a sociable type of way at home. You'll be surprised at how popular your work will be just now and you may just make some money.

Romance and friendship

Expectation is the mother of disappointment and if you've been interacting with a member of the opposite sex via telephone or the Internet, don't expect earth to move under your feet when you meet them between the 3rd and 5th. In fact, this person could turn out to be rather ordinary and not at all what you had anticipated. Oh, well. Back to the drawing board!

Dreams you have on the 8th will be prophetic. You should trust your intuition. Someone may forget an anniversary or important engagement on the 11th and this could make you mad. If you do have something planned, it's not a bad idea to call them to give a gentle reminder of their obligations. A little forethought will spare you later emotional turmoil.

Between the 11th and the 13th you mustn't stop your partner attempting something you think is ridiculous or even dangerous. They may be bored and need stimulation. If you project your own fears on them, and they restrain themselves to satisfy you, you will only be causing them to suppress their natural instincts. Support them in their endeavours, as wild and wacky as they may seem.

On the home front, a problem is brewing with a sibling or neighbour. Be prepared to deal with this around the 16th. Nip this in the bud by taking more time to get to know them a little better.

A friend will be a in a state of confusion between the 20th and the 23rd and it is up to you to help them resolve a rather harrowing situation. There could be an illness and they may not be able to afford the costs. Your compassion will settle them down but don't be drawn into helping them financially. It is their responsibility.

Work and money

Confrontational women at work will be issue for you between the 6th and the 9th, but you mustn't let them get under your skin. You know the type: they know better, they want you to do things their way, and even if you do, it they still aren't satisfied. You need to be a saint with these individuals otherwise you'll do something you will regret. We are only human.

Speaking up is the only way you'll gain the support you desire on the 14th. For fear of upsetting the apple cart you have bitten your tongue for way too long in a situation that you realise must change ASAP. You may not know it but there are others who feel exactly as you do and you have their support. Fearlessness is your key word.

You have your foot on both the brake and the accelerator at the same between the 17th and the 20th. You have to decide one way or the other which way you want to go. There's no point in procrastinating because time will be scarce. This involves pressure from two or perhaps more parties. Weigh up the pros and cons before making your decision.

Destiny dates

Positive: 10, 14, 15, 24, 25, 26, 27, 28, 29, 30

Negative: 2, 16

Mixed: 3, 4, 5, 6, 7, 8, 9, 11, 12, 13, 17, 18, 19, 20, 21, 22, 23

SEPTEMBER

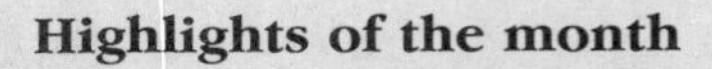

Highlights of the month

You don't necessarily have to retreat this month if you feel that your responsibilities are getting the better of you. No doubt the intense combination of the Sun and Saturn will test your metal. Authority figures will demand more of you than is fair. Deal with it. From the 3rd to the 6th you will feel as if the world is moving in slow motion and your plans are grinding to a halt. Work could seem tedious and unrewarding. This is part of the lesson of Sun and Saturn this month.

Again, Mercury moves into retrogression and creates confusion for you if you rush madly into any agreements or contracts. It's always best to postpone purchases and other commitments until this planet is back on track. That doesn't happen until the last couple of days of the month. Don't feel pressured into making decisions, especially with the above planetary conditions making you feel oppressed.

As a means of overcoming your lethargy or boredom, you may opt to do something extravagant around the 11th. Spending big or partying hard might seem like an escape route but this is only a temporary measure and you will still be left with issues staring you in the face. I'm not saying you shouldn't have some fun but don't for a minute think that this will somehow magically eliminate your problems. This month is about dealing with your problems head-on and not being too discouraged. That is the beauty of astrology. It can at least show you the timeline and when things will improve.

Necessity is the mother of invention so you must always look at the upside. There are opportunities to create something out of nothing between the 15th and the 17th. You'll see things from a completely new perspective at this time and will realise that things are not quite as bad as they seemed. The full intensity of the Sun and Saturn conjunction will occur around the 18th, after which you will feel less stressed and more in control of your life.

Relationships after the 21st are intense and possibly obsessive. This can be the case if there is someone new in your life and you just can't seem to get them out of your head. The feeling may be mutual. Both of you may be SMSing and e-mailing each other to the point of distraction. Your work may suffer even though your romantic feelings will put you on cloud nine.

An important get-together around the 30th will fast track your career and also provide you with plenty of entertainment. You can feel a sigh of relief at the end of this month, that's for sure.

Romance and friendship

You and a loved one perceive a situation from completely different perspectives between the 3rd and the 7th, so why would it surprise you that you can't possibly agree on a solution? Both of you need to step into each other's shoes to look at things from another angle. This means temporarily setting aside your ego and by doing so you'll see how wrong both of you have been. There is a possible third solution to this issue that you have overlooked. It could come to light by the 11th.

Your mind is either your best friend or worst enemy and on the 13th you'll probably feel this more acutely than normal. If you're regurgitating a thought over something someone said without addressing the issue, this revolving door of useless thinking will continue to haunt you. You need to make that call and set the record straight by the 19th.

You need time to adjust to the way a friend is expecting you to think and act. Up till now you may have been amused by some of this person's wild and unpredictable antics. But, by the 21st you'll be in a situation that demands a 'for or against' stance. This will actually be an opportunity for you to see how much respect that they have for you by allowing you to be who you are.

Someone will take advantage of you around the 25th or 26th and it will probably too late to do anything about it. You can't change the past but you can learn from your errors and take extra precautions so that this doesn't happen again in future. At the worst, you will probably feel a little foolish by not having seen it coming. You will not see this person again, either. Just as well.

Work and money

Your financial circumstances will improve by the 4th, but this could have a downside to it. If your savings are accumulating interest, you will have to deal with taxation issues and must minimise your bill to pay the government. There are always ways and means of reducing your tax but it does take a little know-how, preferably through the use of a professional.

If you're thinking of asking for a pay rise you mustn't be too impulsive between the 12th and 15th. Get your facts together before madly rushing into your boss's office and demanding what you think is a fairer deal. They may retaliate with some quite good points you're not aware of. If you flounder, you may lose a valuable opportunity. Scout the territory first before attacking.

You may have a bright idea but if you don't have the allies or support to help implement your concepts it could be an uphill battle. Sometimes enemies turn out to be friends, too, as hard as this may be to swallow. Carefully analyse your options on the 19th and don't be afraid to try something out of the ordinary in your work by the 24th.

Destiny dates

Positive: 16, 17, 18, 19, 24, 30

Negative: 3, 5, 6, 7, 25, 26

Mixed: 4, 11, 12, 13, 14, 15, 21

Highlights of the month

In contrast to last month, the motion of the Sun returning to Libra will catapult your emotions to a high once again. Other planets such as Mercury, Mars and Jupiter also contribute to a better feeling in every department of your life.

Between the 4th and the 9th there is push and shove with Mars providing you extra fuel to achieve a great deal in your work. Problems with co-workers will be resolved after the 5th due to mutually sensitive discussions. You may also be called upon to mediate for several other people because of your impartial attitude. Your sign of Libra is of course represented by the scales of justice and diplomacy.

There are even greater opportunities for you to play a key role in your work as a leader or trendsetter after the 11th. Friendships are invigorated but if they are not pulling their weight in reciprocating their love and time you won't be embarrassed about saying something to them. Telling it as it is will be a feature of your character this month. Your diplomacy may take a back seat.

Some interesting planetary phenomena take place around the 14th. Venus and Mars bring you warmth, vitality and popularity in your relationships. These planets also make you feel rather sexy and attractive to the opposite sex. From the middle of the month you could expect a lift in the personal areas of your life, with some promise being delivered around the 17th.

At this time a close friend could make a pass and this might surprise you as you're not expecting this from them. Slow and steady is the name of the game at this time. If you see this person more as a brother or sister, it will be very difficult to take this friendship to an intimate level. You will have to be careful in breaking the news to them because you don't want to break their heart as well.

Finances are very motivating from the 23rd to the 27th. Making an extra effort to earn as much as possible is your main objective leading up to Christmas. This will occupy your attention and will take you out of the social loop for a while. You will regain your vitality and overcome any minor ailments that have been bothering you due to the physically revitalising Mars.

One of the most excellent planetary combinations of the 29th is that of Venus and Jupiter bringing you a touch of unexpected luck. You may receive a gift or some other token or gesture of goodwill from someone, which touches your heart. There may not be any particular reason for them doing so other than a feeling of appreciation for some help rendered in the past.

Romance and friendship

You are challenged to redefine your philosophical viewpoints due to an unusual change in circumstances on the 2nd. What used to be right and wrong is shifting due to a complex series of events in your life. Of course, you mustn't compromise your standards, but you need to be flexible enough to get through this.

Quick responses are not the best way to deal with someone who is being difficult between the 8th and the 13th. A neighbour or close relative who seems to think that calling the shots and your bowing down to them is how it must be. You need to stand up and assert yourself before you become the victim. You actually have more power than you think.

You may have to help someone you don't particularly like on the 15th or 16th and this will test your spiritual development. There may be no escaping a social situation. You can be civil, pleasant, and leave it at that. You needn't feel obliged to do any more. A higher degree of respect is gained through aloofness on your part—not by sucking up to everyone just because they have a little popularity.

You can be clever about the way you enhance your living circumstances between the 23rd and the 26th, even if you don't have the money to move into something more palatial. Space seems to be the issue now and, if you look closely at how you have organised or arranged your furnishings and other domestic objects, there is certainly more than meets the eye. You can be more intelligent in the way you lay out things. You'll be surprised at how much space you can create.

You can finally begin a new exercise regime by the 28th as health will again be a priority for you.

Work and money

Your initial reaction to suggestions of change may not be warranted around the 8th. A second thought on the advice you receive shows it has more merit than you think if you analyse it more carefully. Don't be so impulsive, listen to what is said and then weigh up your options. There could be a bigger opportunity than you had at first suspected.

It's annoying when bureaucrats give you mixed signals between the 10th and the 15th. You will be tearing your hair out trying to solve what should really be a simple problem. You could spend inordinate amounts of time on the telephone, sending e-mails or basically a driving yourself crazy. You may just have to let the universe solve this rather than bang your head against the wall.

You're restless between the 20th and 24th and need to be out and about rather than deskbound. You may be delayed making the break, but once you do you'll feel refreshed and ready to party this weekend. It is one of those days where you may choose to pat yourself on the back and take an early mark. Why not? You probably deserve it. The following few days bring exciting and challenging events.

Destiny dates

Positive: 4, 5, 6, 7, 17, 20, 21, 22, 23, 24, 25, 26, 27, 28, 29

Negative: 2

Mixed: 8, 9, 10, 11, 12, 13, 14, 15, 16

NOVEMBER

Highlights of the month

Money fascinates you this month, but if you're still experiencing a few dilemmas that can't be solved, you mustn't let your stubbornness and pride interfere with timely advice that you might receive from someone much more experienced than you are. On the 2nd and the 3rd you'll be actively engaged in working through partnerships—personal and professional—and at some point money could become a sore point.

A blend of good conversational skills and well-researched information is necessary. If you want others to help you improve your financial status, you really need to know what you want. If you are airy-fairy and can't advise them on what you need, how can they do the job for you? This is why you need to analyse carefully your immediate, medium- and long-term goals this month.

You'll want to use your creativity in your friendships and, between the 8th and 13th, you will want to spring a surprise on friends just for the shock–comic value if nothing else. This will introduce an element of fun to the group and, if you've been finding the patterns of relating becoming a little stale, this is a great way to kick-start your social scene again.

Throughout the 14th to the 17th you will want to make such a strong impression that you overlook the fact that you can't deliver on your promises. It's important for you to be realistic during this cycle and remember that the solution you're looking for may not be an overnight panacea. Take into account other factors and what others think on the matter as well. This will be the case particularly between the 18th and the 21st when discussions with relatives require more listening on your part. Read between the lines if others are sharing their thoughts.

Circumstances out of your control are a test of your ability to go with the flow. Someone who likes to dominate the situation will be pushing you to your limits. Saturn and Pluto are in a very tight and difficult aspect and this is highlighted around the 16th. Coupled with this you may be confused as to how to react. Should you come out and speak your mind, or bide your time and wait to see what eventuates? When Mercury favours you around the 19th you're in a better position to address this issue with the person in question, but not before.

The conjunction of Venus and Uranus after the 26th promises a romantic surprise. For some Librans, marriage is now not out of the question. Someone may pop the question or at least take your relationship to the next level in readiness for the big event.

Romance and friendship

Occasionally the package, the presentation of a person, seems perfect—almost too perfect. If your intuition sets alarm bells ringing about the true character of a person you happen to meet on the 2nd, trust it completely. You smell a rat and the person probably is!

Between the 5th and the 9th you'll discover you have a secret admirer and probably don't even really believe it. There may have been some hints and some possible suspicions on your part but, even if there were, you may not be able to put two and two together. If you were to find out who it is, it could be rather embarrassing. Wouldn't you be surprised to find that it is probably a partner or a friend of a good friend? Let's just leave it at that.

Inequity in your relationships around the 12th means you're the one putting up the greater amount of effort. Relationships must be mutually satisfying and you will be feeling as if your partner has to start pulling their weight for it to be worthwhile in the end. Habits become more ingrained over time. A leopard doesn't change its spots that easily, so remember that.

Taking the time to show your appreciation via e-mails or simple telephone calls will pay handsome dividends between the 22nd and the 27th. In modern times the idea of a thank you note or a token of gratitude has fallen by the wayside. These small acts will differentiate you from others and win you some unforeseen popularity as a result.

On the 29th tell your partner about their character and how they should treat you in intimate moments, even if this is difficult for you at first. The truth is hard to tell but will stimulate important changes to the better.

Work and money

If you're taking on a greater share of the workload and haven't said anything about it, why would others stop shoving more work on your desk? If you are dissatisfied with your working arrangement on the 7th and others continue to take you for a ride, you need to say something rather than becoming the pack horse for your work group.

You could develop an interest in psychic phenomena between the 13th and the 15th. If you have had some vague plan to earn money or make a career through this practice, you need to be patient as the fruits are often a long way off until you build up a clientele and also a half-decent reputation. Practise on your friends and family members and keep a record of the results. This is the best way to become talented in this field.

An overreaction on your part will make matters worse financially between the 27th and the 29th. The secret is to keep your cool and not jump to conclusions over bills. You may find that an invoice is not correct, so don't fret. Make the right call to the appropriate person and the matter will be solved quickly.

Destiny dates

Positive: 3, 5, 6, 8, 9, 10, 11, 13, 22, 23, 24, 25, 26

Negative: 28

Mixed: 2, 7, 12, 14, 15, 16, 17, 18, 19, 20, 21, 27, 29

DECEMBER

Highlights of the month

As the year draws to a close, Saturn will impact upon the horoscope of most Librans by remaining in their Sun sign for at least two-and-a-half years. Important decisions will need to be made as you become more serious about your life and in particular your work. Just as a snake as sheds its skin, you too will start to find that certain aspects of your life now need to be jettisoned for you to be successful. Between the 3rd and the 9th, do what needs to be done and don't feel obliged to explain the ins and outs of your own personal process. It really isn't anyone else's business.

It's not a bad idea to lighten things up by actively engaging yourself in some fun, social events. The new Moon of the 16th and the entry of Venus into your third zone of travels, communications and day-to-day living, will take a load off your shoulders. Involve yourself in artistic pursuits, dance and other creative pleasures.

Around the 19th someone who has gained power by force or nebulous means may be exposed. Someone you know may be caught out in a lie. Your investigative work will be the source of this revelation. If you are meeting new people, especially online, please take care that you don't automatically assume that they are people of integrity. Test the waters first, especially before meeting them in person.

As Christmas looms Mars moves retrograde, indicating that you may not have the physical energy or desire to take in the usual madness that is often associated with this time of the year. Between the 17th and the 21st you will prefer to remain incognito and, although you know that you will probably make a rod for your own back by not going out and doing your Christmas shopping or sending obligatory Christmas cards, you'll still prefer to play the waiting game.

That will all change when Venus moves into your zone of family affairs on the 26th. You will again want to get involved with the family and proactively involve yourself in the festivities. As Venus remains in this position of the rest of the month, it promises to be a thoroughly happy Christmas period for you.

On the 27th to the 30th I think the best suggestion I can make for you is to put aside the serious issues that are lurking deep in the recesses of your mind and simply enjoy the Christmas season without too much stress. You will gain some clarity from simple pleasures this month and this seems the best way for you to make your transition into 2010 as easy and fulfilling as possible. Forget your cares and enjoy yourself.

Romance and friendship

Between the 5th and the 9th you could be worried about telling someone an uncomfortable truth about themselves. You know what I mean: perhaps their body odour is offensive or an aspect of their behaviour is grating on other people's nerves. Until you say something you're going to feel annoyed about it.

If you try to keep up with modern fads, especially jargon that just doesn't fit with who you are as a person, you'll trip up yourself. If you are in the company of others around the 14th, just be yourself. Be proud of who you are. You'll gain their respect and this will take the pressure off you as well.

Your humour will win you friends between the 19th and 24th and a relaxed state of mind will prevail. This will help you rest, work and play more comfortably. If telling a few jokes works for you, make it a permanent feature of your life.

Don't build up plans around someone changeable in nature because they may let you down at the last minute by the 21st. If you have an inkling that someone is unreliable, then don't place too much expectation on them. It's likely you'll receive a call just before the appointment and be blown off once again.

A change of residence, even if it is only temporary, is a welcome relief this month. The 24th and 25th are dates on which you may travel or momentarily relocate. If you choose to house sit, make sure the terms of engagement are clear so that you avoid misunderstandings at the end of your stay.

A new relationship moves into top gear by the 29th. You can start to really inspire each other. There are good omens for this friendship becoming something quite special. Expect some breakthrough in communication. This is a lucky period for love.

Work and money

You may know exactly what you want on the 9th, with your vision and timing coming together perfectly. A third factor may be a thorn in your side, however, and that is ... money. Unfortunately you need more than is required to obtain this mini-goal. You will need to borrow if you don't want to miss the boat.

The period of the new Moon of the 16th until the 22nd will be focused on getting your work schedule completely in order.

You can devise a new system that will help you shortcut your way to the finishing line and make your workload a lot easier leading up to Christmas. The only thing is the need to make the time to do this planning. Allow for adequate planning time.

If you're feeling ineffectual it's because of two things. The first is that you have not armed yourself with sufficient information or expertise. The second, even if you have the knowledge, is that you are not projecting your desires and willpower into the world around you strongly enough. You need to get both these in sync to make the right sort of impression and you can do so between the 29th and the 31st.

Destiny dates

Positive: 3, 4, 16, 17, 18, 19, 20, 22, 23, 24, 25, 26, 27, 28, 29, 30, 31

Negative: Nil

Mixed: 5, 6, 7, 8, 9, 14, 21

LIBRA

2009: Astronumerology

Our history is not our destiny.

—Alan Cohen

The power behind your name

By adding the numbers of your name you can see which planet is ruling you. Each of the letters of the alphabet is assigned a number, which is tabled below. These numbers are ruled by the planets. This is according to the ancient Chaldean system of numerology and is very different to the Pythagorean system to which many refer.

Each number is assigned a planet:

AIQJY	**=**	**1**	**Sun**
BKR	**=**	**2**	**Moon**
CGLS	**=**	**3**	**Jupiter**
DMT	**=**	**4**	**Uranus**
EHNX	**=**	**5**	**Mercury**
UVW	**=**	**6**	**Venus**
OZ	**=**	**7**	**Neptune**
FP	**=**	**8**	**Saturn**
—	**=**	**9**	**Mars**

Notice that the number 9 is not allotted a letter because it is considered special. Once the numbers have been added you will see that a single planet rules your name and personal affairs. Many famous actors, writers and musicians change their names to attract the energy of a luckier planet. You can experiment with the table and try new names or add letters of your second name to see how that vibration suits you. It's a lot of fun!

Here is an example of how to find out the power of your name. If your name is John Smith, calculate the ruling planet by correlating each letter to a number in the table like this:

J O H N   S M I T H

1 7 5 5   3 4 1 4 5

Now add the numbers like this:

1 + 7 + 5 + 5 + 3 + 4 + 1 + 4 + 5 = 35

Then add 3 + 5 = 8

The ruling number of John Smith's name is 8, which is ruled by Saturn. Now study the name-number table to reveal the power of your name. The numbers 3 and 5 will also play a secondary role in John's character and destiny so in this case you would also study the effects of Jupiter and Mercury.

Name-number table

Your name number	Ruling planet	Your name characteristics
1	Sun	Charismatic personality. Great vitality and life force. Physically active and outgoing. Attracts good friends and individuals in powerful positions. Good government connections. Intelligent, dramatic, showy and successful. A loyal number for relationships.
2	Moon	Soft, emotional temperament. Changeable moods but psychic, intuitive senses. Imaginative nature and compassionate expression of feelings. Loves family, mother and home life. Night owl who probably needs more sleep.

		Success with the public and/or the opposite sex.
3	Jupiter	Outgoing, optimistic number with lucky overtones. Attracts opportunities without trying. Good sense of timing. Religious or spiritual aspirations. Can investigate the meaning of life. Loves to travel and explore the world and people.
4	Uranus	Explosive personality with many quirky aspects. Likes the untried and untested. Forward thinking, with many unusual friends. Gets bored easily so needs plenty of stimulating experiences. Innovative, technological and creative. Wilful and stubborn when wants to be. Unexpected events in life may be positive or negative.
5	Mercury	Quick-thinking mind with great powers of speech. Extremely active life; always on the go and lives on nervous energy. Youthful attitude and never grows old. Looks younger than actual age. Young friends and humorous disposition. Loves reading and writing.
6	Venus	Charming personality. Graceful and attractive character, who cherishes friends and social life. Musical or artistic interests. Good for money making as well as numerous love affairs. Career in

		the public eye is possible. Loves family but is often overly concerned by friends.
7	Neptune	Intuitive, spiritual and self-sacrificing nature. Easily duped by those who need help. Loves to dream of life's possibilities. Has healing powers. Dreams are revealing and prophetic. Loves the water and will have many journeys in life. Spiritual aspirations dominate worldly desires.
8	Saturn	Hard-working, focused individual with slow but certain success. Incredible concentration and self-sacrifice for a goal. Money orientated but generous when trust is gained. Professional but may be a hard taskmaster. Demands highest standards and needs to learn to enjoy life a little more.
9	Mars	Incredible physical drive and ambition. Sports and outdoor activities are keys to health. Combative and likes to work and play just as hard. Protective of family, friends and territory. Individual tastes in life but is also self-absorbed. Needs to listen to others' advice to gain greater success.

Your 2009 planetary ruler

Astrology and numerology are closely linked. Each planet rules over a number between 1 and 9. Both your name and your birth date are ruled by planetary energies. Here are the planets and their ruling numbers:

1 Sun; 2 Moon; 3 Jupiter; 4 Uranus; 5 Mercury; 6 Venus; 7 Neptune; 8 Saturn; 9 Mars

Simply add the numbers of your birth date and the year in question to find out which planet will control the coming year for you. Here is an example:

If you were born on 12 November, add the numerals 1 and 2 (12, your day of birth) and 1 and 1 (11, your month of birth) to the year in question, in this case 2009 (current year), like this:

Add 1 + 2 + 1 + 1 + 2 + 0 + 0 + 9 = 16

Then add these numbers again: 1 + 6 = 7

The planet ruling your individual karma for 2009 will be Neptune because this planet rules the number 7.

You can even take your ruling name number as shown above and add it to the year in question to throw more light on your coming personal affairs like this:

John Smith = 8

Year coming = 2009

Add 8 + 2 + 0 + 0 + 9 = 19

Add 1 + 9 = 10

Add 1 + 0 = 1

This is the ruling year number using your name number as a basis. Therefore, study the Sun's (number 1) influence for 2009. Enjoy!

1 = Year of the Sun

Overview

The Sun is the brightest object in the heavens and rules number 1 and the sign of Leo. Because of this the coming year will bring you great success and popularity.

You'll be full of life and radiant vibrations and are more than ready to tackle your new nine-year cycle, which begins now. Any new projects you commence are likely to be successful.

Your health and vitality will be very strong and your stamina at its peak. Even if you happen to have the odd problem with your health, your recuperative power will be strong.

You have tremendous magnetism this year so social popularity won't be a problem for you. I see many new friends and lovers coming into your life. Expect loads of invitations to parties and fun-filled outings. Just don't take your health for granted as you're likely to burn the candle at both ends.

With success coming your way, don't let it go to your head. You must maintain humility, which will make you even more popular in the coming year.

Love and pleasure

This is an important cycle for renewing your love and connections with your family, particularly if you have children. The Sun is connected with the sign of Leo and therefore brings an increase in musical and theatrical activities. Entertainment and other creative hobbies will be high on your agenda and bring you a great sense of satisfaction.

Work

You won't have to make too much effort to be successful this year as the brightness of the Sun will draw opportunities to you. Changes in work are likely and if you have been concerned that opportunities are few and far between, 2009 will be different. You can expect some sort of promotion or an increase in income because your employers will take special note of your skills and service orientation.

Improving your luck

Leo is the ruler of number 1 and therefore, if you're born under this star sign, 2009 will be particularly lucky. For others, July and August, the months of Leo, will bring good fortune. The 1st, 8th, 15th and 22nd hours of Sundays especially will give you a unique sort of luck in any sort of competition or activities generally. Keep your eye out for those born under Leo as they may be able to contribute something to your life and may even have a karmic connection to you. This is a particularly important year for your destiny.

Your lucky numbers in this coming cycle are 1, 10, 19 and 28.

2 = Year of the Moon

Overview

There's nothing more soothing than the cool light of the full Moon on a clear night. The Moon is emotional and receptive and controls your destiny in 2009. If you're able to use the positive energies of the Moon, it will be a great year in which you can realign and improve your relationships, particularly with family members.

Making a commitment to becoming a better person and bringing your emotions under control will also dominate your thinking. Try not to let your emotions get the better of you throughout the coming year because you may be drawn into the changeable nature of these lunar vibrations as well. If you fail to keep control of your emotional life you'll later regret some of your actions. You must carefully blend thinking with feeling to arrive at the best results. Your luck throughout 2009 will certainly be determined by the state of your mind.

Because the Moon and the sign of Cancer rule the number 2 there is a certain amount of change to be expected this year. Keep your feelings steady and don't let your heart rule your head.

Love and pleasure

Your primary concern in 2009 will be your home and family life. You'll be keen to finally take on those renovations, or work on your garden. You may even think of buying a new home. You can at last carry out some of those plans and make your dreams come true. If you find yourself a little more temperamental than usual, do some extra meditation and spend time alone until you sort this out. You mustn't withhold your feelings from your partner as this will only create frustration.

Work

During 2009 your focus will be primarily on feelings and family; however, this doesn't mean you can't make great strides in your work as well. The Moon rules the general public and what you might find is that special opportunities and connections with the world at large present themselves to you. You could be working with large numbers of people.

If you're looking for a better work opportunity, try to focus your attention on women who can give you a hand. Use your intuition as it will be finely tuned this year. Work and career success depends upon your instincts.

Improving your luck

The sign of Cancer is your ruler this year and because the Moon rules Mondays, both this day of the week and the month of July are extremely lucky for you. The 1st, 8th, 15th and 22nd hours on Mondays will be very powerful. Pay special attention to the new and full Moon days throughout 2009.

The numbers 2, 11 and 29 are lucky for you.

3 = Year of Jupiter

Overview

The year 2009 will be a 3 year for you and, because of this, Jupiter and Sagittarius will dominate your affairs. This is very lucky and shows that you'll be motivated to broaden your horizons, gain more money and become extremely popular in your social circles. It looks like 2009 will be a fun-filled year with much excitement.

Jupiter and Sagittarius are generous to a fault and so likewise, your openhandedness will mark the year. You'll be friendly and helpful to all of those around you.

Pisces is also under the rulership of the number 3 and this brings out your spiritual and compassionate nature. You'll become a much better person, reducing your negative karma by increasing your self-awareness and spiritual feelings. You will want to share your luck with those you love.

Love and pleasure

Travel and seeking new adventures will be part and parcel of your romantic life this year. Travelling to distant lands and meeting unusual people will open your heart to fresh possibilities of romance.

You'll try novel and audacious things and will find yourself in a different circle of friends. Compromise will be important in making your existing relationships work. Talk about your feelings. If you are currently in a relationship you'll feel an upswing in your affection for them. This is a perfect opportunity to deepen your love for each other and take your relationship to a new level.

If you're not yet attached to someone just yet, there's good news for you. Great opportunities lie in store for you and a spiritual or karmic connection may be experienced in 2009.

Work

Great fortune can be expected through your working life in the next twelve months. Your friends and work colleagues will want to help you achieve your goals. Even your employers will be amenable to your requests for extra money or a better position within the organisation.

If you want to start a new job or possibly begin an independent line of business this is a great year to do it. Jupiter looks set to give you plenty of opportunities, success and a superior reputation.

Improving your luck

As long as you can keep a balanced view of things and not overdo anything, your luck will increase dramatically throughout 2009. The important thing is to remain grounded and not be too airy-fairy about your objectives. Be realistic about your talents and capabilities and don't brag about your skills or achievements. This will only invite envy from others.

Moderate your social life as well and don't drink or eat too much as this will slow your reflexes and lessen your chances for success.

You have plenty of spiritual insights this year so you should use them to their maximum. In the 1st, 8th, 15th and 24th hours of Thursdays you should use your intuition to enhance your luck, and the numbers 3, 12, 21 and 30 are also lucky for you. March and December are your lucky months but generally the whole year should go pretty smoothly for you.

4 = Year of Uranus

Overview

The electric and exciting planet of the zodiac Uranus and its sign of Aquarius rule your affairs throughout 2009. Dramatic events will surprise and at the same time unnerve you in your professional and personal life. So be prepared!

You'll be able to achieve many things this year and your dreams are likely to come true, but you mustn't be distracted or scattered with your energies. You'll be breaking through your own self-limitations and this will present challenges from your family and friends. You'll want to be independent and develop your spiritual powers and nothing will stop you.

Try to maintain discipline and an orderly lifestyle so you can make the most of these special energies this year. If unexpected things do happen, it's not a bad idea to have an alternative plan so you don't lose momentum.

Work

Technology, computing and the Internet will play a larger role in your professional life this coming year. You'll have to move ahead with the times and learn new skills if you want to achieve success.

A hectic schedule is likely, so make sure your diary is with you at all times. Try to be more efficient and don't waste time.

New friends and alliances at work will help you achieve even greater success in the coming period. Becoming a team player will be even more important towards gaining satisfaction in your professional endeavours.

Love and pleasure

You want something radical, something different in your relationships this year. It's quite likely that your love life will be feeling a little less than exciting so you'll take some important steps to change that. If your partner is as progressive as you'll be this year, then your relationship is likely to improve and fulfil both of you.

In your social life you will meet some very unusual people whom you'll feel are specially connected to you spiritually. You may want to ditch everything for the excitement and passion of a completely new relationship, but tread carefully as this may not work out exactly as you'd expected.

Improving your luck

Moving too quickly and impulsively will cause you problems on all fronts, so be a little more patient and think your decisions through more carefully. Social, romantic and professional opportunities will come to you but take a little time to investigate the ramifications of your actions.

The 1st, 8th, 15th and 20th hours of any Saturday are lucky, but love and luck are likely to cross your path when you least expect it. The numbers 4, 13, 22 and 31 are also lucky for you this year.

5 = Year of Mercury

Overview

The supreme planet of communication, Mercury, is your ruling planet throughout 2009. The number 5, which is connected to Mercury, will confer upon you success through your intellectual abilities.

Any form of writing or speaking will be improved and this will be, to a large extent, underpinning your success. Your imagination will be stimulated by this planet with many incredible new and exciting ideas will come to mind.

Mercury and the number 5 are considered somewhat indecisive. Be firm in your attitude and don't let too many ideas or opportunities distract and confuse you. By all means get as much information as you can to help you make the right decision.

I see you involved with money proposals, job applications, even contracts that need to be signed so remain clear-headed as much as possible.

Your business skills and clear and concise communication will be at the heart of your life in 2009.

Love and pleasure

Mercury, which rules the signs of Gemini and Virgo, will make your love life a little difficult due to its changeable nature. On the one hand you'll feel passionate and loving to your partner, yet on the other you will feel like giving it all up for the excitement of a new affair. Maintain the middle ground.

Also, try not to be too critical with your friends and family members. The influence of Virgo makes you prone to expecting much more from others than they're capable of giving. Control your sharp tongue and don't hurt people's feelings. Encouraging others is the better path, leading to more emotional satisfaction.

Work

Speed will dominate your professional life in 2009. You'll be flitting from one subject to another and taking on far more than you can handle. You'll need to make some serious changes in your routine to handle the avalanche of work that will come your way. You'll also be travelling with your work, but not necessarily overseas.

If you're in a job you enjoy then this year will give you additional successes. If not, it may be time to move on.

Improving your luck

Communication is the secret of attaining your desires in the coming twelve months. Keep focused on one idea rather than scattering your energies in all directions and your success will be speedier.

By looking after your health, sleeping well and exercising regularly, you'll build up your resilience and mental strength.

The 1st, 8th, 15th and 20th hours of Wednesday are lucky so it's best to schedule your meetings and other important social engagements during these times. The lucky numbers for Mercury are 5, 14, 23 and 32.

6 = Year of Venus

Overview

Because you're ruled by 6 this year, love is in the air! Venus, Taurus and Libra are well known for their affinity with romance, love, and even marriage. If ever you were going to meet a soulmate and feel comfortable in love, 2009 must surely be your year.

Taurus has a strong connection to money and practical affairs as well, so finances will also improve if you are diligent about work and security issues.

The important thing to keep in mind this year is that sharing love and making that important soul connection should be kept high on your agenda. This will be an enjoyable period in your life.

Love and pleasure

Romance is the key thing for you this year and your current relationships will become more fulfilling if you happen to be attached. For singles, a 6 year heralds an important meeting that eventually leads to marriage.

You'll also be interested in fashion, gifts, jewellery and all sorts of socialising. It's at one of these social engagements that you could meet the love of your life. Remain available!

Venus is one of the planets that has a tendency to overdo things, so be moderate in your eating and drinking. Try generally to maintain a modest lifestyle.

Work

You'll have a clearer insight into finances and your future security during a number 6 year. Whereas you may have had additional expenses and extra distractions previously, your mind will be more settled and capable of longer-term planning along these lines.

With the extra cash you might see this year, decorating your home or office will give you a special sort of satisfaction.

Social affairs and professional activities will be strongly linked. Any sort of work-related functions may offer you romantic opportunities as well. On the other hand, be careful not to mix up your workplace relationships with romantic ideals. This could complicate some of your professional activities.

Improving your luck

You'll want more money and a life of leisure and ease in 2009. Keep working on your strengths and eliminate your negative personality traits to create greater luck and harmony in your life.

Moderate all your actions and don't focus exclusively on money and material objects. Feed your spiritual needs as well. By balancing the inner and outer you'll see that your romantic and professional life will be enhanced more easily.

The 1st, 8th, 15th and 20th hours on Fridays will be very lucky for you and new opportunities will arise for you at those times. You can use the numbers 6, 15, 24 and 33 to increase luck in your general affairs.

7 = Year of Neptune

Overview

The last and most evolved sign of the zodiac is Pisces, which is ruled by Neptune. The number 7 is deeply connected with this zodiacal sign and governs you in 2009. Your ideals seem to be clearer and more spiritually orientated than ever before. Your desire to evolve and understand your inner self will be a double-edged sword. It depends on how organised you are as to how well you can use these spiritual and abstract concepts in your practical life.

Your past emotional hurts and deep emotional issues will be dealt with and removed for good, if you are serious about becoming a better human being.

Spend a little more time caring for yourself rather than others, as it's likely some of your friends will drain you of energy with their own personal problems. Of course, you mustn't turn a blind eye to the needs of others, but don't ignore your own personal needs in the process.

Love and pleasure

Meeting people with similar life views and spiritual aspirations will rekindle your faith in relationships. If you do choose to develop a new romance, make sure that there is a clear understanding of the responsibilities of one to the other. Don't get swept off your feet by people who have ulterior motives.

Keep your relationships realistic and see that the most idealistic partnerships must eventually come down to Earth. Deal with the practicalities of life.

Work

This is a year of hard work, but one in which you'll come to understand the deeper significance of your professional ideals. You may discover a whole new aspect to your career, which involves a more compassionate and self-sacrificing side to your personality.

You'll also find that your way of working will change and that you'll be more focused and able to get into the spirit of whatever you do. Finding meaningful work is very likely and therefore this could be a year when money, security, creativity and spirituality overlap to bring you a great sense of personal satisfaction.

Tapping into your greater self through meditation and self-study will bring you great benefits throughout 2009.

Improving your luck

Using self-sacrifice along with discrimination will be an unusual method of improving your luck. The laws of karma state that what you give, you receive in greater measure. This is one of the principal themes for you in 2009.

The 1st, 8th, 15th and 20th hours of Tuesdays are your lucky times. The numbers 7, 16, 25 and 34 should be used to increase your lucky energies.

8 = Year of Saturn

Overview

The earthy and practical sign of Capricorn and its ruler Saturn are intimately linked to the number 8, which rules you in 2009. Your discipline and farsightedness will help you achieve great things in the coming year. With cautious discernment, slowly but surely you will reach your goals.

It may be that due to the influence of the solitary Saturn, your best work and achievement will be behind closed doors away from the limelight. You mustn't fear this as you'll discover many new things about yourself. You'll learn just how strong you really are.

Love and pleasure

Work will overshadow your personal affairs in 2009, but you mustn't let this erode the personal relationships you have. Becoming a workaholic brings great material successes but will also cause you to become too insular and aloof. Your family members won't take too kindly to you working 100-hour weeks.

Responsibility is one of the key words for this number and you will therefore find yourself in a position of authority that leaves very little time for fun. Try to make time to enjoy the company of friends and family and by all means schedule time off on the weekends as it will give you the peace of mind you're looking for.

Because of your responsible attitude it will be very hard for you not to assume a greater role in your workplace and this indicates longer working hours with the likelihood of a promotion with equally good remuneration.

Work

Money is high on your agenda in 2009. Number 8 is a good money number according to the Chinese and this year is at last likely to bring you the fruits of your hard labour. You are cautious and resourceful in all your dealings and will not waste your hard-earned savings. You will also be very conscious of using your time wisely.

You will be given more responsibilities and you're likely to take them on, if only to prove to yourself that you can handle whatever life dishes up.

Expect a promotion in which you will play a leading role in your work. Your diligence and hard work will pay off, literally, in a bigger salary and more respect from others.

Improving your luck

Caution is one of the key characteristics of the number 8 and is linked to Capricorn. But being overly cautious could cause you to miss valuable opportunities. If an offer is put to you, try to think outside the square and balance it with your naturally cautious nature.

Be gentle and kind to yourself. By loving yourself, others will naturally love you, too. The 1st, 8th, 15th and 20th hours of Saturdays are exceptionally lucky for you as are the numbers 1, 8, 17, 26 and 35.

9 = Year of Mars

Overview

You are now entering the final year of a nine-year cycle dominated by the planet Mars and the sign of Aries. You'll be completing many things and are determined to be successful after several years of intense work.

Some of your relationships may now have reached their use-by date and even these personal affairs may need to be released. Don't let arguments and disagreements get in the road of friendly resolution in these areas of your life.

Mars is a challenging planet and, this year, although you will be very active and productive, you may find others trying to obstruct the achievement of your goals. As a result you may react strongly to them, thereby creating disharmony in your workplace. Don't be so impulsive or reckless, and generally slow things down. The slower, steadier approach has greater merit this year.

Love and pleasure

If you become too bossy and pushy with friends this year you will just end up pushing them out of your life. It's a year to end certain friendships but by the same token it could be the perfect time to end conflicts and thereby bolster your love affairs in 2009.

If you're feeling a little irritable and angry with those you love, try getting rid of these negative feelings through some intense, rigorous sports and physical activity. This will definitely relieve tension and improve your personal life.

Work

Because you're healthy and able to work at a more intense pace you'll achieve an incredible amount in the coming year. Overwork could become a problem if you're not careful.

Because the number 9 and Mars are infused with leadership energy, you'll be asked to take the reins of the job and steer your company or group in a certain direction. This will bring with it added responsibility but also a greater sense of purpose for you.

Improving your luck

Because of the hot and restless energy of the number 9, it is important to create more mental peace in your life this year. Lower the temperature, so to speak, and decompress your relationships rather than becoming aggravated. Try to talk to your work partners and loved ones rather than telling them what to do. This will generally pick up your health and your relationships.

The 1st, 8th, 15th and 20th hours of Tuesdays are the luckiest for you this year and, if you're involved in any disputes or need to attend to health issues, these times are also very good for the best results. Your lucky numbers are 9, 18, 27 and 36.

LIBRA

2009: Your Daily Planner

> *A man's mind may be likened to a garden, which may be intelligently cultivated or allowed to run wild; but whether cultivated or neglected, it must, and will, bring forth.*
>
> —James Allen

There is a little-known branch of astrology called electional astrology, and it can help you select the most appropriate times for many of your day-to-day activities.

Ancient astrologers understood the planetary patterns and how they impacted on each of us. This allowed them to suggest the best possible times to start various important activities. Many farmers today still use this approach: they understand the phases of the Moon, and attest to the fact that planting seeds on certain lunar days produces a far better crop than planting on other days.

The following section covers many areas of daily life, and uses the cycles of the Moon and the combined strength of the other planets to work out the best times to start different types of activity.

So to create your own personal almanac, first select the activity you are interested in, and then quickly scan the year for the best months to start it. When you have selected the month, you can finetune your timing by finding the best specific dates. You can then be sure that the planetary energies will be in sync with you, offering you the best possible outcome.

Coupled with what you know about your monthly and weekly trends, the daily planner can be a powerful tool to help you capitalise on opportunities that come your way this year.

Good luck, and may the planets bless you with great success, fortune and happiness in 2009!

Starting activities

How many times have you made a new year's resolution to begin a diet or be a better person in your relationships? And how many times has it not worked out? Well, the reason may be partly that you started out at the wrong time! How successful you are is strongly influenced by the position of the Moon and the planets when you begin a particular activity. You could be more successful with the following activities if you start them on the days indicated.

Relationships

We all feel more empowered on some days than on others. This is because the planets have some power over us—their movement and their relationships to each other determine the ebb and flow of our energies. And our level of self-confidence and our sense of romantic magnetism play an important part in the way we behave in relationships.

Your daily planner tells you the ideal dates for meeting new friends, initiating a love affair, spending time with family and loved ones—it even tells you the most appropriate times for sexual encounters.

You'll be surprised at how much more impact you make in your relationships when you tune yourself in to the planetary energies on these special dates.

Falling in love/restoring love

During these times you could expect favourable energies to meet your soulmate or, if you've had difficulty in a relationship, to approach the one you love to rekindle both your and their emotional responses:

January	28, 30
February	25, 26
March	6, 7, 8, 28, 29, 30
April	25, 26, 30
May	1, 2, 5, 7, 26, 27, 28, 29

June	2, 3, 23, 24, 26, 29, 30
July	22, 23, 26, 27
August	14, 15, 16, 17, 22, 23, 24
September	10, 14, 16, 19, 20, 21
October	9, 10, 11, 12, 13
November	25, 26
December	22, 23, 27, 31

Special times with friends and family

Socialising, partying and having a good time with those you enjoy being with is highly favourable under the following dates. These dates are excellent to spend time with family and loved ones in a domestic environment:

January	26
February	8, 12, 13, 14, 22, 23, 24
March	8, 22, 23
April	19, 27, 28
May	1, 2, 15, 16, 17, 24, 25, 28, 29
June	2, 3, 11, 12, 13, 22, 30
July	23, 26, 27
August	5, 6, 23, 24
September	16
October	13
November	8, 10, 24
December	19, 20, 21, 29

Healing or resuming relationships

If you're trying to get back together with the one you love and need a heart-to-heart or deep and meaningful, you can try the following dates to do so:

February	8, 12, 13, 14
March	8
April	18, 19
May	1, 2, 28, 29
June	2, 3, 30
July	23, 26, 27
August	23, 24
September	16
October	13
November	8
December	22, 23, 27

Sexual encounters

Physical and sexual energies are well favoured on the following dates. The energies of the planets enhance your moments of intimacy during these times:

January	5, 30
February	25, 26
March	6, 7, 8, 28, 29, 30
April	25, 26, 30
May	1, 2, 5, 7, 26, 27, 28, 29
June	2, 3, 23, 24, 26, 29, 30

July	22, 23, 26, 27
August	23, 24
September	16
October	13
November	25, 26
December	22, 23, 27, 31

Health and wellbeing

Your aura and life force are susceptible to the movements of the planets; in particular, they respond to the phases of the Moon.

The following dates are the most appropriate times to begin a diet, have cosmetic surgery, or seek medical advice. They also tell you when the best times are to help others.

Feeling of wellbeing

Your physical as well as your mental alertness should be strong on these following dates. You can plan your activities and expect a good response from others:

January	8, 9, 26, 27
February	4, 5, 22, 23
March	31
April	18, 19, 27, 28
May	16, 17
June	21, 22
July	19
August	5, 6, 24, 25
September	12, 28, 30

October	8, 9
November	8, 10
December	19, 20, 21, 29, 30

Healing and medicine

This is good for approaching others who have expertise at a time when you need some deeper understanding. This is also favourable for any sort of healing or medication and making appointments with doctors or psychologists. Planning surgery around these dates should bring good results.

Often giving up our time and energy to assist others doesn't necessarily result in the expected outcome. By lending a helping hand to a friend on the following dates, the results should be favourable:

January	1, 20, 21, 22, 23, 24, 25, 26, 27, 28, 29, 30, 31
February	9, 10, 11, 12, 13, 14, 15, 16, 17, 18, 19, 20, 21, 22, 23, 24, 25, 26, 27, 28
March	2, 3, 4, 5, 6, 7, 8, 9, 22, 26, 28, 29, 30, 31
April	1, 10, 12, 15, 18, 20, 27, 28, 29, 30
May	1, 3, 7, 8, 9, 10, 11, 12
June	6, 7, 9, 13, 14, 15, 19, 21, 22
July	5, 6, 7, 8, 10, 12, 18, 19, 20, 25, 26
August	6, 7, 8, 9, 10, 29, 30, 31
September	1, 6, 27
October	8, 9, 10, 11, 12, 25, 26
November	18, 19, 20, 21, 22
December	10, 11, 12

Money

Money is an important part of life, and involves many decisions; decisions about borrowing, investing, spending. The ideal times for transactions are very much influenced by the planets, and whether your investment or nest egg grows or doesn't grow can often be linked to timing. Making your decisions on the following dates could give you a whole new perspective on your financial future.

Managing wealth and money

To build your nest egg, it's a good time to open your bank account and invest money on the following dates:

January	3, 4, 5, 10, 11, 16, 17, 23, 24, 25, 31
February	1, 6, 7, 12, 13, 14, 20, 21, 27, 28
March	5, 6, 7, 12, 13, 19, 26, 27
April	2, 3, 8, 9, 15, 17, 23, 24, 29, 30
May	5, 6, 7, 13, 14, 20, 21, 26, 27
June	2, 3, 9, 10, 16, 17, 18, 23, 24, 29, 30
July	6, 7, 8, 14, 15, 20, 21, 26, 27
August	2, 3, 4, 10, 11, 17, 18, 23, 24, 30, 31
September	6, 7, 13, 14, 19, 20, 26, 27
October	3, 4, 5, 10, 11, 16, 17, 18, 23, 24, 25, 31
November	1, 6, 7, 13, 14, 20, 21, 27, 28
December	4, 5, 10, 11, 17, 18, 24, 25, 26, 31

Spending

It's always fun to spend but the following dates are more in tune with this activity and are likely to give you better results:

January	20, 28, 30
February	3
March	28, 29, 30
April	25, 26
May	31
June	1, 2, 7, 8, 9, 10, 28, 30
July	1, 2, 3, 26, 27, 29, 30
August	2, 3, 4, 5, 20, 21, 22, 23, 24, 25
September	19, 20, 21, 22, 23
October	9, 10
November	1, 7, 8, 17
December	27, 28

Selling

If you're thinking of selling something, whether it is small or large, consider the following dates as ideal times to do so:

January	3, 18, 19, 20, 21, 25, 26, 27, 28, 29, 30, 31
February	8, 10, 11, 12, 13, 14, 15, 18, 20, 22, 23, 24, 26, 28
March	2, 3, 4, 5, 6, 7, 8, 9, 16, 26, 27, 28, 31
April	5, 10, 19, 20, 23, 25, 27, 28, 29
May	1, 2, 7, 9, 13, 14, 21, 24, 25, 28, 29, 31
June	1, 2, 7, 8, 14, 16, 17, 20, 21, 22, 26, 30
July	1, 2, 3, 9, 10, 11, 15, 16, 17, 26, 27
August	2, 3, 4, 13, 14, 15, 16, 17
September	1, 2, 3, 4, 5, 6, 14, 15, 16, 17, 21, 22, 23, 24, 25, 26, 27, 28, 30, 31

October	1, 2, 3, 4, 5, 6, 7, 8, 9, 10, 11, 12, 31
November	2, 3, 9, 10, 11, 12, 13, 25, 26, 27, 28, 29, 30
December	1, 2, 3, 7, 8, 9, 17, 20

Borrowing

Few of us like to borrow money, but if you must, taking out a loan on the following dates should be positive:

January	11, 18, 19, 20, 23, 24, 25
February	15, 16, 20, 21
March	14, 15, 19, 20
April	10, 11, 12, 15, 16, 17
May	9, 13, 14
June	9, 10
July	7, 8, 20, 21
August	17, 18
September	13, 14
October	10, 11
November	6, 7, 15, 16
December	4, 5, 12, 13, 14

Work and education

Your career is important to you, and continual improvement of your skills is therefore also crucial, professionally, mentally and socially. The dates below will help you find out the most appropriate times to improve your professional talents and commence new work or education associated with your work.

You may need to decide when to start learning a new skill, when to ask for a promotion, and even when to make an important career change. Here are the days when mental and educational power is strong.

Learning new skills

Educational pursuits are lucky and bring good results on the following dates:

January	8, 9
February	4, 5
March	3, 4, 10, 31
April	1, 6, 7, 27, 28
May	3, 4, 25, 30, 31
June	1, 6, 7, 27, 28
July	4, 5, 24, 25, 31
August	1, 21, 22, 27, 28, 29
September	23, 24, 25
October	21, 22
November	17, 18, 19
December	29, 30

Changing career path or profession

If you're feeling stuck and need to move into a new professional activity, changing jobs can be done at these times:

January	6, 7
February	2, 3
March	1, 2, 3, 4, 5, 6, 7, 8, 9, 10, 28, 29, 30
April	6, 7, 25, 26
May	3, 4, 30, 31
June	1, 27, 28

July	6, 24, 25
August	2, 3, 4, 21, 22, 30, 31
September	26, 27
October	23, 24, 25
November	2, 20, 21, 29, 30
December	1, 17, 18, 27, 28

Promotion, professional focus and hard work

To increase your mental focus and achieve good results from the work you do, promotions are likely on these dates that follow:

January	4, 5, 6, 11, 12, 13, 14, 15, 16, 21
February	6
March	18, 19, 20
April	8, 28, 29
May	12, 21
June	25, 26
July	1, 2, 3, 8, 15, 17
August	4, 14, 15, 16, 17, 18, 22, 23, 24
September	14, 15, 18, 19, 23, 24, 25, 26
October	22
November	7, 10, 11, 12, 17
December	1, 2, 3, 7, 28

Travel

Setting out on a holiday or adventurous journey is exciting. To gain the most out of your holidays and journeys, travelling on the following dates is likely to give you a sense of fulfilment:

January	9, 10, 28, 29, 30, 31
February	1, 4, 5, 26
March	3, 4, 5, 6, 7, 27, 31
April	27, 28, 29
May	1, 2, 25
June	6, 7, 25, 26
July	6, 31
August	1, 2, 21, 22, 23, 24, 29
September	19, 20, 23, 24, 25, 26, 27
October	1, 2, 3, 25, 28, 29, 30, 31
November	1, 17, 18, 26, 28
December	17, 18, 23, 26

Beauty and grooming

Believe it or not, cutting your hair or nails has a powerful effect on your body's electromagnetic energy. If you cut your hair or nails at the wrong time of the month, you can reduce your level of vitality significantly. Use these dates to ensure you optimise your energy levels by staying in tune with the stars.

Hair and nails

January	1, 2, 8, 9, 21, 22, 28, 29, 30
February	4, 5, 17, 18, 19, 25, 26
March	3, 4, 16, 17, 18, 24, 25, 31
April	1, 13, 14, 20, 21, 22, 27, 28, 29, 30
May	8, 10, 11, 12, 18, 19, 24, 25
June	6, 7, 8, 14, 15, 21, 22

July	4, 5, 11, 12, 13, 18, 19, 31
August	1, 7, 8, 9, 14, 15, 16, 27, 28, 29
September	4, 5, 11, 12, 23, 24, 25
October	1, 2, 8, 9, 21, 22, 28, 29, 30
November	4, 5, 17, 18, 19, 25, 26
December	2, 3, 15, 16, 22, 23, 29, 30

Therapies, massage and self-pampering

January	18, 19, 20, 26, 27
February	3, 6, 7, 8, 12, 13, 14, 15, 16, 22, 23, 24
March	6, 8, 28, 29, 30
April	5, 8, 9, 18, 19, 25, 26, 29, 30
May	1, 2, 5, 7, 9, 15, 16, 17, 22, 23, 26, 27, 28, 29
June	2, 3, 4, 5, 11, 12, 13, 19, 20, 23, 24, 26, 30
July	1, 2, 3, 9, 10, 23, 26, 27, 28, 29, 30
August	6, 12, 13, 17, 18, 19, 20, 23, 24, 25, 26
September	1, 2, 13, 14, 16
October	10, 11, 12, 13, 16, 17, 27
November	8, 9, 10, 13, 16, 23, 24, 29, 30
December	1, 4, 5, 6, 7, 10, 11, 12, 13, 14, 19, 20, 21, 27, 28, 31